James Grant Wilson

Mr. Secretary Pepys

With extracts from his diary

James Grant Wilson

Mr. Secretary Pepys
With extracts from his diary

ISBN/EAN: 9783337124229

Printed in Europe, USA, Canada, Australia, Japan

Cover: Foto ©Andreas Hilbeck / pixelio.de

More available books at **www.hansebooks.com**

MR. SECRETARY PEPYS:

WITH

EXTRACTS FROM HIS DIARY.

By ALLAN GRANT.

New York:

PUBLICATION OFFICE, BIBLE HOUSE.

JAMES PORTEUS, AGENT.

1867.

STEREOTYPED AT THE
BOSTON STEREOTYPE FOUNDRY,
4 Spring Lane.

TO THE

WIFE OF A DISTINGUISHED UNITED STATES SENATOR,

A CHRISTIAN LADY, ALIKE BEAUTIFUL IN MIND AND PERSON,

WHO MINISTERED TO A WOUNDED BROTHER,

STRICKEN UNTO DEATH ON THE FATAL FIELD OF FREDERICKSBURG,

This Little Volume is Dedicated,

BY HER MOST GRATEFUL AND ATTACHED FRIEND,

THE AUTHOR.

So long they read in those antiquities,
That how the time was fled they quite forgate.

EDMUND SPENSER.

They are the
Registers, the chronicles of the age
They were made in, and speak the truth of history.

SHAKERLY MARMION.

An exact Diary is a window into his heart that maketh it; and therefore pity it is that any should look therein but either the friends of the party, or such ingenious foes as will not (especially in things doubtful) make conjectural comments to his disgrace.

PRYNNE'S REMARKS ON ARCHBISHOP LAUD.

MR. SECRETARY PEPYS.

AMONG the many glimpses into the life and manners of the olden time, to the reflecting and philosophic mind few are so deeply interesting as the daily memoranda of eminent men long since passed from the stage; those patient and disinterested benefactors of posterity, who have at stated seasons stolen away from the troublous and anarchical scenes of busy existence, and in the lull of strife, and it may be of suffering and bloodshed, have daily devoted a few sacred and precious moments to photographing the stirring events of the day — records that fill us no less with wonder at the uniqueness and beauty of their coloring, than with admiration of the stern truth and fidelity of the incidents detailed.

(5)

With the Diarist there is no stage room for loftiness of port or histrionic swagger — he indulges in no flatulent outbreak of patriotism no yeasty rodomontade of national glory. His heroes are ushered on the stage with no alarums of jubilant trumpets — no roll of martial drums ; but at a chosen hour, you tranquilly sit down with him as with a beloved old crony of long standing, and you listen to his calm and brief story, mayhap of some solemn life narrative of sorrow and vicissitude, which he quietly details to you with the steady flow of a clear but deep stream, which often murmurs but never brawls, and to whose soothing music you unreluctantly surrender for the time all the regrets of the past, all the anxieties of the future.

The historian may narrate events deeply riveting in their nature — matters of great pith and moment germain to the public weal and prosperity of the time. He may balance nice questions of statesmanship, unravel knotty skeins of shrewd diplomacy, or successfully sift conflicting evidence on recondite points of international law. But he lives remote from the men and things he would describe, must write from the authority of those who have preceded him, and can offer no better warrant for his averments than what he finds already written by those who may have as slight foundation for their facts as he has for his personal knowledge of their veracity.

Now, the value of all this historical merit is heavily overborne by the diarist who has not only had an intimate knowledge of the actors in his drama, but has, in all probability, himself been one of the *dramatis personæ*, and taken either a leading or subordinate part throughout the entire representation. Moreover, the minute accuracy of the *stippling* (to use an artistic term), breadth of handling, and truth of detail exemplified by our best Diarists, incontestably prove the painters to have been as faithful delineators as they were careful observers of the scenes they portray — scenes "all which they saw, and part of which they were." History, which a wag asserts to mean *his story*, is now manufactured in this country not by the book, but by the bale; and so prolific have these historical scribblers become, that we may soon expect to see histories sold by the box, like India rubber shoes or pegged boots and brogans. Again, like true cannibals, these bookmakers have at length come to live upon each other, and carve, serve up, and rehash each other's inanities *ad*

infinitum, and all to earn an ephemeral reputation and turn an honest penny into two pennies
not just so honest.

A writer of this tribe may be false in his
premises, fallacious in his reasoning, and pre-
posterous in his conclusions ; he may, in the estimation of all sensible and intelligent men, be
at best a mere historical *chiffonnière* — a resur-
rectionist of forgotten facts and thrice demolished
fictious — a renovator of defunct chronicles and
all the rubbish garnered up by learned associa-
tions styling themselves " Societies."   With
wondrous industry and persevering diligence he
rakes these *disjecta membra* together — these
sweepings of a study — sifts, riddles, and re-
adjusts to suit the taste of the time, and of a
given accumulation of such ill-considered trifles
he makes a book, names it a History, and, with
a crow much akin to a cackle, he calls upon
the world to wonder and worship.   Many may
think the book a good book, but to your true
student and scholar it has a *blague* second-
hand look about it, something like an old seedy
black coat which some colored pusson of your
acquaintance has re-buttoned, sponged, and
" goosed up," till it looks almost as good as
new.   To historians such as Schlosser, Macau-

lay, Thiers, Carlyle, Prescott, Bancroft, and Motley, we willingly doff the literary beaver, and as cheerfully render homage due to genius, learning, character, and respectability; our feud is only with the ignoble pack of paltry imitators, who perseveringly foist their counterfeit wares on a long-suffering and patient public — curs of whose historical yelpings the world has long been sick and weary. Let us now turn to worthy old Samuel Pepys, a bird of quite a different feather.

Many of our readers may not even have heard of Samuel Pepys — Pepys, the son of a London tailor, and the prince of journalists, who has embalmed for posterity such a world of blended gossip and historical fact, that for many years has proved to the student of English history a perfect treasure-trove, which we feel assured said posterity will not willingly let die.

Apart from his Diary all the information relative to his family and personal history is meagre and unsatisfactory. From the recent discovery of an old manuscript journal belonging to the great uncle of the Journalist, we are enabled to trace his family to a remote period. This curious book was found by the Rev. John Dale, vicar of Bolney, Sussex, England, in

March, 1852, in an ancient chest in his parish church, and contains, *inter alia*, the following entry: " A Noate written out of an ould Booke of my uncle William Pepys." " William Pepys died at Cotterham, 10 H. 8, was brought up by the Abbat of Crowland in Huntingdonshire, and he was borne in Dunbar in Scotland, a gentleman whom the said Abbat did make his bayliffe of all his lands in Cambridgeshire and placed him in Cottinham. Which William aforesaid had three sons, Thomas, John and William, to whom Margaret was mother naurallie, all of whom left issue." Samuel Pepys, grandson of Thomas just mentioned, was born at Bampton, Huntingdonshire, on the 23d day of February, 1632-3, received his education at St. Paul's School, and at Magdalen College, Cambridge.

The only record of his college career is the following: " October 21, 1653. Pepys and Hind were solemnly admonished by myself and Mr. Hill, for being scandalously overserved with drink the night before. This was done in the presence of all the Fellows then resident. John Wood, Reg'r." Two years later he married Elizabeth St. Michael, whose father, a Frenchman, accompanied Queen Henrietta Maria to England as one of her suite. The marriage seems to have been a sufficiently happy one, though nothing could easily be more rash. He was but twenty-three, and his wife fifteen, and neither of them had property. How the London tailor's son came to be related to so distinguished a person as Sir Edward Montagu, we are not told : but so it was ; and in the house of that distinguished officer the young couple found an asylum, and to the connection thus accidentally formed Pepys owed his successful career.

Being patronized by his cousin, Sir Edward, afterwards the first Earl of Sandwich, he accompanied him as secretary in the fleet that was sent to bring back Charles the Second. Pepys was in high favor with the monarch, and introduced many important improvements into the navy. On the accession of William and Mary, he published his " Memoirs " relating to the navy — a valuable work. Independent of his great skill and experience in naval affairs, he was well informed in history, painting, sculpture, architecture, and kindred arts. Such indeed was his reputation, that in 1684 he was made president of the Royal · Society.

But that which has most contributed to give an interest to the name of Pepys, of late years,

is the recent publication of his Diary, which,
besides illustrating his own wary and prudent
character with so much truthfulness and naïveté,
affords a curious and instructive picture of the
court of the merry monarch, and gives an
interesting view of the manners and habits
of the people at large. Living as he did in an
eventful age, and at an era teeming and rich
beyond measure with remarkable incidents and
characters, it was fortunate for the world that
Pepys undertook a task for which he was so
admirably fitted, a task which, after all, to him
seemed but a pleasant duty. To arrest, and as
it were embalm, the passing characters and
transactions of his time, and transmit them in
all their glowing and life-like freshness of coloring, was no mean bequest to posterity; and
whatever be its other claims to the respect and
admiration of the reading world, as a simple
verification of history it is invaluable.

The celebrated John Evelyn was a brother
diarist of Pepys : they were also old friends and
correspondents, and to be the friend of Evelyn
was no slight compliment to the character and
accomplishments of Pepys; and Collier, the author of a Biographical Dictionary, and a contemporary, in an affectionate notice of his death

speaks of him in the following glowing terms :
" It may be affirmed of this gentleman that he
was without exception the greatest and most
useful minister that ever filled the same situa-
tions in England ; the acts and registers of the
Admiralty proving this fact beyond contradic-
tion. The principal rules and establishments
in present use in those offices are well known
to have been of his introducing, and most of
the officers serving therein since the Restoration, of his bringing up.

He was a most studious promoter and strenu-
ous assertor of order and discipline through all
their dependencies. Sobriety, diligence, capacity, loyalty, and subjection to command, were
essentials required in all whom he advanced.
Where any of those were found wanting, no
interest or authority was capable of moving
him in favor of the highest pretender, the
royal command only excepted, of which he was
also very watchful to prevent any undue pro-
curements.

Discharging his duty to his prince and country with a religious application and perfect
integrity, he feared no one, and courted no one,
and neglected his own fortune. Besides this he
was a person of universal worth, and in great

estimation among the literati for his unbounded
reading, his sound judgment, his great elocu-
tion, his mastery in method, his singular curiosity, and his uncommon munificence towards
the advancement of learning, arts, and industry
in all degrees ; to which were joined the severest
morality of a philosopher, and all the polite
accomplishments of a gentleman, particularly
those of music, languages, conversation, and
address.   He assisted as one of the Barons of
the Cinque Ports at the coronation of James
the Second, and was a standing Governor of
all the principal houses of charity in and about
London, and sat at the head of many other
honorable bodies, in divers of which, as he
deemed their constitution and methods deserv-
ing, he left lasting monuments of his bounty
and patronage."

The Diary begins at that interesting period
subsequent to the death of Cromwell, and while
the whole country was in a state of deep agita-
tion, as the question of *King or no King* began
to absorb the public mind.   Like Alexander's
captains, after the great Macedonian had laid
down the burden of empire and existence together, there was an ominous gathering spirit
of *sauve qui peut* apparent among the parlia-

mentary generals, that betokened some approaching disruption in the forces under their command. The heavy ground swell in the political
ocean had not yet subsided, and thoughtful and
observant men began to look with anxiety for
the lifting up of the curtain that concealed the
coming year, and in whose impenetrable folds
seemed hidden events that would speedily decide
the fate of the kingdom. The iron hand of
Cromwell was forever at rest, but the iron rule
and the stern despotism still remained. The
government of the sword had not yet lost its
prestige, and men still trembled as with furtive
look and bated breath they gathered into obscure
nooks to discuss the probable action of Monk,
who, at the head of the forces in Scotland, now
appeared to hold the destiny of England in his
hand. Monk was the master-spirit among the
military leaders of the Parliamentary army,
talked loudly of the Commonwealth, free Par-
liaments, and the people's right, and at York
caned one of his officers for charging him with
attempting the restoration of the king ; and yet
his plans were matured to effect this very object, and he only staid the developments of time
to announce to the country that its lawful monarch waited in a foreign port for its recognition

of his claims and a speedy recall to his crown and native country.

Fairfax, always at heart a royalist, held back, and, seeming to bide his time, calmly waited for the coming man. Fleetwood chafed and blustered, and finally on his knees surrendered his commission to the speaker of the House. Such was the general aspect of things at the period at which Pepys began his Diary, and we shall now leave the further detail of events to him.

Diary of Samuel Pepys.

1659–60.

" Blessed be God, at the end of the last year I was in very good health, without any sense of my old pain, but upon taking of cold. I lived in Axe Yard, having my wife and servant Jane, and no other in family but us three.

The condition of the State was thus, viz.: the Rump, after being disturbed by my Lord Lambert,[1] was lately returned to sit again. The officers of the army are forced to yield.

---

1 Sufficiently known by his services as a major-general in the Parliament forces during the civil war, and condemned as a traitor after the Restoration, but reprieved and banished to Guernsey, where he lived in confinement thirty years.

Lawson [1] lies still in the river, and Monk [2] is with his army in Scotland. Only my Lord Lambert is not yet come into the Parliament, nor is it expected that he will, without being forced to it. The new Common Council of the city do speak very high ; and had sent to Monk, their sword-bearer, to acquaint him with their desires for a free and full Parliament, which is at present the desires and the hopes, and the expectations of all ; twenty-two of the old secluded members having been at the House door the last week to demand entrance, but it was denied them ; and it is believed that neither they nor the people will be satisfied till the House be filled. My own private condition very handsome, and esteemed rich, but indeed very poor ; besides my goods of my house, and my office, which is somewhat certain. Mr. Downing [3] master of my office.

January 1*st*. (Lord's Day.) This morning (we living lately in the garret) I rose, put on my suit with great skirts, having not lately worn

---

[1] Sir John Lawson, who rose to the rank of an admiral, and greatly distinguished himself during the protectorate of Oliver Cromwell.

[2] George Monk, afterwards Duke of Albemarle.

[3] Afterwards Sir George Downing, son of Emmanuel Downing, a London merchant who settled in New England.

any other clothes but them.   Went to Mr. Gun-
ning's chapel at Exeter House, where he made
a very good sermon upon these words: 'That
in the fulness of time God sent his Son, made
of a woman,' &c.; showing that by 'made
under the law' is meant the circumcision, which
is solemnized this day.   Dined at home in the
garret, where my wife dressed the remains of a
turkey, and in doing it she burned her hand.   I
stayed at home the whole afternoon, looking
over my accounts; then went with my wife to
my father's, and in going observed the great
posts which the City workmen set up at the
Conduit in Fleet Street.

2d. Walked a great while in Westminster
Hall, where I heard that Lambert was coming
up to London; that my Lord Fairfax[1] was in
the head of the Irish brigade, but it was not
certain what he would declare for.   The House
was to-day upon finishing the act for the Council of State, which they did; and for the indemnity of the soldiers; and were to sit again
thereupon in the afternoon.   Great talk that
many places had declared for a free Parlia-

---

[1] Thomas Lord Fairfax, generalissimo of the Parliamentary
forces. After the Restoration, he retired to his country-seat,
where he lived in private till his death in 1671.

ment; and it is believed that they will be forced
to fill up the House with the old members.
From the Hall I called at home, and so went to
Mr. Crewe's (my wife she was to go to her
father's), and Mr. Moore and I and another
gentleman went out and drank a cup of ale
together in the New Market, and there I eat
some bread and cheese for my dinner.

3*d.* To White Hall, where I understood that
the Parliament had passed the act of indemnity
for the soldiers and officers that would come in,
in so many days, and that my Lord Lambert
should have benefit of the said act. They had
also voted that all vacancies in the House, by the
death of the old members, should be filled up;
but those that are living shall not be called in.

4*th.* Strange the difference of men's talk.
Some say that Lambert must of necessity yield
up; others, that he is very strong, and that the
Fifth-monarchy men will stick to him, if he
declares for a free Parliament. Chillington was
sent yesterday to him with the note of pardon
and indemnity from the Parliament. Went and
walked in the Hall, where I heard that the Parliament spent this day in fasting and prayer;
and in the afternoon came letters from the
North, that brought certain news that my Lord

Lambert his forces were forsaking him, and
that he was left with only fifty horse, and that
he did now declare for the Parliament himself;
and that my Lord Fairfax did also rest satisfied,
and has laid down his arms, and that what he
had done was only to secure the country against
my Lord Lambert his raising money and free
quarter. I met with the clerk and quarter-
master of my Lord's troop, and Mr. Jenkins
showed me two bills of exchange for money to
receive upon my Lord's and my pay.

5th. I dined with Mr. Shepley, at my Lord's
lodgings, upon his turkey-pie. And so to my
office again; where the Excise money was
brought, and some of it told to soldiers till it
was dark. Then I went home, after writing to
my Lord the news that the Parliament had
this night voted that the members that were
discharged from sitting in the years 1648 and
49 were duly discharged; and that there should
be writs issued presently for the calling of
others in their places, and that Monk and Fairfax were commanded up to town, and that the
President Bradshaw's [1] lodgings were to be provided for Monk at Whitehall. Then my wife
and I, it·being a great frost, went to Mrs.

---

[1] John Bradshaw, president of the High Court of Justice.

Jem's,[1] in expectation to eat sack-posset, **but**
Mr. Edward not coming, it was put off; **and I**
left my wife playing at cards with her, and went
myself to Mr. Fage, to consult concerning my
nose, who told me it was nothing **but** a cold.
Mr. Fage and I did discourse concerning public
business; and he told me it is true the **city had**
not time enough to do much, but they **are re-**
solved **to** shake off the soldiers; and that unless there be a free Parliament chosen, he did
believe there are half the Common Council will
not levy any money **by** order **of this Parlia-**
ment.

6th. This **morning Mr. Shepley and I** did
eat our breakfast **at Mrs.** Harpers (my brother
John[2] being with me) **upon a cold turkey-pie**
and a goose. **At my** office where we paid
money to the soldiers till one o'clock; **and I**
took my wife to my cosen Thomas Pepys, **and**
found them **just sat down to** dinner which **was**
very good; only **the venison** pastry was **palpa-**
ble mutton, which was **not handsome.**"

Very true, neither handsome nor honest, **and**
making **it** apparent that there were shams **in**
England before Carlyle's **day.** It also **reminds**

[1] Jemimah, daughter of Sir Edward Montagu.
[2] John Pepys, afterwards in holy orders; died 1677.

us of the remark of an irreverent grumbler at a New York boarding-house table more famed for its pretensions to gentility than for the quality or plentifulness of its viands : "Mrs. Jenkins, if this were not called beef steak, I should have taken it for fried liver."

At the conclusion of our last extract, we left Pepys growling over the indignity of being fobbed off with mutton for venison, which was an unquestionably shabby transaction. This leads us to contrast the mode of living in that day and that of our present year of grace 1867. In relation to a dinner he gave to a select party of friends, or rather relations, in which he says, " My company was my father, my uncle Fenner and his two sons, Mr. Pierce, and all their wives, and my brother Tom," he details the different dishes with a gusto and precision which prove him to have been an ardent lover of good cheer.

Here everything is plain, nutritious, and abundant, and utterly free from kickshaws and flummery of every kind — and the honest, wholesome simplicity of the repast is sadly at issue with the costly and elaborate artificiality of the household dinners perpetrated in the present day. Mrs. Pepys' dish of marrow bones — the leg of mutton and loin of veal — were beyond question super-excellent, each in its own way; but the magnificent idea of the " three pullets, and the dozen sky-larks, all in a dish," was the crowing glory of the *chef de cuisine,* and must have formed a feature in the symposium worthy of Alexis Soyer or Pierre Blot in their happiest moments of inspiration.

Then the decent propriety and English solidity of the dessert is worthy of our highest respect and admiration — the " great tart," the " neat's tongue " — ah, that neat's tongue ! embalmed in anchovies, " like a dish of swate strawberries smothered in crame," and scarcely to be eclipsed by those dark ruby prawns, and the deep red double-Gloster cheese, ever as grateful to the palate as it is pleasant to the eye. This grand family banquet sans doubt, was doubly enhanced by copious libations of stout, old, home-brewed, brown October, in big-bellied jugs, black jacks, and foaming flagons, that merrily coursed round the hospitable board, till the black oaken rafters rang with " Down with the Rump, and speedy restoration to King Charles ! "

It has frequently been remarked that whether a birth or a funeral takes place in a household,

the great business of eating and drinking goes
on with the same steady uniformity as if no such
event had transpired.   In confirmation of this
truth we have Pepys and his friends on more
than one occasion holding *high jinks*, and enjoy-
ing themselves with more than Spartan stoi-
cism of mind, in times of deep anxiety and distress — a strong evidence, by the way, of their
good sense, and belief that there is no special
wisdom in caring for the morrow, and that
enough for the day is the evil thereof.

Monk, the ephemeral Napoleon of the day,
having outmanœuvred his military rivals, was
marching on the city with his invincible bat-
talions, the heroes of a hundred fights.   The
pay of these forces was deeply in arrear, and
it was muttered throughout the ranks that if
pay was not to be obtained, plunder could ; and
they were likely to make good the threat.   Let
it be remembered, these were no carpet war-
riors ; no trim, highly-tailored militiamen, come
out to air their finery on parade, but men of
iron mould and iron purpose ; Cromwell's right
arm and right hand, that raised up and struck
down all opposing powers at his bidding ;
psalm-singing soldiers, who looked upon the
day of battle as a day of certain victory, and

who, now grown to be an army of mutinous, red-handed dictators, were approaching the metropolis of the land to right their **own** wrongs, and *take* justice should **it** chance to be denied them.

This threat set prudent householders **to** stow away their valuables, burying them in cellars, gardens, and other by-corners, till these armed malcontents were amicably compromised with ; hence, in taking down old houses in London, it was a common occurrence to find money, jewels, and other valuable effects, concealed in walls, cellars, and secret nooks throughout the dwelling, whose owners, in the interim, having died, the treasures had never been reclaimed. Now for a few **more life-sketches from** Samuel Pepys : —

"13*th*. Coming in the morning to my office, I met Mr. Fage, and took him to the Swan.[1] He told me how he, Haselrigge,[2] and Morley,[3]

---

[1] Fenchurch Street, **London.**

[2] **Sir Arthur Haselrigge, Bart.,** of Nosely, Leicester County, and member of Parliament for that county; colonel of a regiment **in the Parliament army,** and much esteemed by Cromwell. In March **following he was** committed to the Tower, where he died, January, 1660–61. He was brother-in-**law** to Lord Brooke, who was killed at Lichfield.

[3] **Probably Colonel Morley, Lieutenant of the** Tower, **whom Evelyn blames so strongly** for not doing **what** Monk did.

the last night, began at my Lord Mayor's,[1] to exclaim against the city of London, saying that they had forfeited their charter; and how the Chamberlain of the city did take them down, letting them know how much they were formerly holden to the city, &c. He told me that Monk's letter that came by the sword-bearer, was a cunning piece, and that which they did not much trust to; but they were resolved to make no more applications to the Parliament, nor pay any money unless the secluded members be brought in, or a free Parliament chosen. To Mrs. Jem, and found her up and merry, as it did not prove the small-pox, but the swine-pox; so I played a game or two of cards with her.

16th. In the morning I went up to Mr. Crewe's, who did talk to me concerning things of State; and expressed his mind how just it was that the secluded members should come to sit again. From thence to my office, where nothing to do; but Mr. Downing came and found me all alone; and did mention to me his going back into Holland, and did ask me whether I would go or no, but gave me little

[1] Sir Thomas Allen, created a baronet at the Restoration. He was ruined by his expenses as Lord Mayor.

encouragement, but bid me consider of it; and asked me whether I did not think that Mr. Hawley could perform the work of my office alone. I confess that I was at a great loss all the day after to bethink myself how to carry this business. I staid up till the bell-man came by with his bell just under my window as I was writing of this very line, and cried, ' Past one of the clock, and a cold, frosty, windy morning.'

17*th*. In our way to Kensington we understood how that my Lord Chesterfield had killed another gentleman about half an hour before, and was fled. I went to the coffee club (Miles's), and heard very good discourse; it was in answer to Mr. Harrington's answer, who said that the state of the Roman government was not a settled government, and so it was no wonder that the balance of the prosperity was in one hand, and the command in another, it being therefore always in a posture of war; but it was carried by ballot that it was a steady government, though it is true by the voices that it had been carried before that it was an unsteady government; so to-morrow it is to be proved by the opponents that the balance lay in one hand, and the government in another. Thence I went to Westminster, and met Shaw and Washington, who told me how this day, Sydenham was voted out of the House for sitting any more this Parliament, and that Salloway was voted out likewise and sent to the Tower, during the pleasure of the House. At Harper's, Jack Price told me, among other things, how much the Protector is altered; though he would seem to bear out his trouble very well, yet he is scarce able to talk sense with a man; and how he will say that 'who should a man trust, if he may not trust to a brother and an uncle;' and 'how much these men have to answer before God Almighty, for their playing the knave with him as they did.' He told me also, that there was £100,000 offered, and would have been taken for his restitution, had not the Parliament come in as they did again; and that he do believe that the Protector will live to give a testimony of his valor and revenge yet before he dies, and that the Protector will say so himself sometimes.

18*th*. I interpreted my Lord's letter by his character.[1] All the world is at a loss to think what Mouk will do; the City saying that he

---

[1] i. e., in cipher.

will be for them, and the Parliament saying he will be for them.

22d. (Lord's Day). To church in the afternoon to Mr. Herring, where a lazy, poor sermon. This day I began to put on buckles to my shoes.

23d. This day the Parliament sat late, and resolved of the declaration to be printed for the people's satisfaction, promising them a great many good things. In the garden of White Hall, going through to the Stone Gallery, I fell in a ditch, it being very dark.

24th. I took my wife to Mr. Pierce's,[1] she, in her way, being exceedingly troubled with a pair of new pattens, and I vexed to go so slow, it being late. We found Mrs. Carrick very fine, and one Mr. Lucy, who called one another husband and wife, and after dinner a great deal of mad stir. There was pulling off Mrs. Bride's and Mr. Bridegroom's ribbons, and a great deal of fooling among them that I and my wife did not like. Mr. Lucy and several other gentlemen coming in after dinner, swearing and singing as if they were mad, only he singing very handsomely. There also came in Mr. (James)

---

[1] James Pierce, surgeon to the Duke of York, and husband of the pretty Mrs. P., whose name occurs so often in the jovial Secretary's journal.

Southerne, clerk to Mr. Blackburn, and with him Lambert, lieutenant of my Lord's ship, and brought with them the declaration that came out to-day from the Parliament, wherein they declare for law and gospel and for tythes; but I do not find people apt to believe them. This day the Parliament gave orders that the late Committee of Safety should come before them this day se'nnight, and all their papers, and their model of government that they had made, to be brought in with them. Mr. Crumlum gave my father directions what to do about getting my brother an exhibition, and spoke very well of him.

25th. Coming home, heard that in Cheapside there had been but a little before a gibbet set up, and the picture of Huson [1] hung upon it, in

[1] John Hewson, who, from a low origin, became a colonel in the Parliament army, and sat in judgment on the king: he escaped hanging by flight, and died, in 1662, at Amsterdam. A curious notice of Hewson occurs in Rugge's Diurnal, 5th December, 1659, which states that " he was a cobbler by trade, but a very stout man, and a very good commander; but in regard of his former employment, they (the city apprentices) threw at him old shoes, and slippers, and turnip-tops, and brickbats, stones, and tiles." . . . . " At this time (January, 1659–60), there came forth, almost every day, jeering books; one was called Colonel Hewson's Confession, or a Parley with Pluto, about his going into London, and taking down the gates of Temple-bar." He had but one eye, which did not escape the notice of his enemies.

the middle of the street. I called at Paul's churchyard, where I bought Buxtor's Hebrew Grammar, and read (at Kirton's) a declaration of the gentlemen of Northampton, which came out this afternoon. To Mr. Crewe's about a picture to be sent into the country, of Thomas Crewe, to my Lord.

26*th.* Called for some papers at Whitehall for Mr. Downing, one of which was an Order of the Council for £1800 per annum, to be paid monthly; and the other two, Orders to the Commissioners of Customs, to let his goods pass free. Home from my office to my Lord's lodgings, where my wife had got ready a very fine dinner, viz: a dish of marrow bones, a leg of mutton, a loin of veal, a dish of fowl, three pullets, and a dozen of larks, all in a dish; a great tart, a neat's tongue, a dish of anchovies, and a dish of prawns and cheese. My company was my father, my uncle Fenner, his two sons, Mr. Pierce, and all their wives, and my brother Tom. The news this day is a letter that speaks absolutely Monk's concurrence with this Parliament, and nothing else, which yet I hardly believe. I wrote two characters for Mr. Downing and carried them to him."

Pepys was not only a good singer, who could

enhance the flavor of a cup of sack with a
" mighty funny story," or a " most admirable
song," but also composed several airs of great
beauty.   On the 30th, he says, " This morning
before I was up I fell a-singing of my song,
' Great, good, and just,' &c., and put myself
thereby in mind that this was the fatal day, now
ten years since his Majesty died."   This song,
the first words of which are quoted, was written
on the execution of Charles the First (and probably set to music by Pepys) by one of the
most gallant soldiers of the seventeenth century
— the Marquis of Montrose, who, among all the
great men of his age, in the opinion of the Car-
dinal de Retz, approached most nearly to the
ancient heroes of Greece and Rome.   In addi-
tion to his reputation as an illustrious commander, it may truly be said that he possessed an
elegant genius, spoke eloquently, and wrote
with a graceful and perspicuous style.   The
night before his execution at the age of thirty-
eight, he composed, in his prison, the verses that
follow : —

" Let them bestow on every airth a limb,
    Open all my veins, that I may swim
    To thee, my Saviour, in that crimson lake,
    Then place my parboiled head upon a stake,

Scatter my ashes, throw them in the air;
Lord, since thou know'st where all these atoms are,
I'm hopeful once thou'lt recollect my dust,
And confident thou'lt raise me with the just."

The lines which THE GREAT MARQUIS, as he was called by his contemporaries, composed on the execution of his royal friend, and which Pepys designates as " my song," are, —

" Great, good, and just, could I but rate
My grief and thy too rigid fate,
I'd weep the world to such a strain
That it should deluge once again.
But since thy loud-tongued blood demands supplies
More from Briareus' hands than Argus' eyes,
I'll sing thy obsequies with trumpet sounds,
And write thy epitaph with blood and wounds."

" *February* 1st. Took Gammer East, and James the porter, a soldier, to my Lord's lodgings, who told me how they were drawn into the field to-day, and that they were ordered to march away to-morrow, to make room for General Mouk; but they did shout their Colonel Fitch [1] and the rest of the officers out of the field, and swore they would not go without their money, and if they would not give it

---

1 Thomas Fitch, colonel of a regiment of foot, in 1658 M. P. for Inverness; he was also Lieutenant of the Tower of London.

them, they would go where they might have it, and that was the city. So the Colonel went to the Parliament, and commanded what money could be got, to be got against to-morrow for them, and all the rest of the soldiers in town, who in all places made a mutiny this day, and do agree together.

2nd. To my office, where I found all the officers of the regiment in town waiting to receive money, that their soldiers might go out of town, and what was in the Exchequer they had. Harper, Luellin, and I, went to the Temple, to Mr. Calthrop's chamber, and from thence had his man by water to London Bridge, to Mr. Calthrop, a grocer, and received £60 for my Lord. In our way, we talked with our waterman, White, who told us how the watermen had lately been abused by some that had a desire to get in to be watermen to the State, and had lately presented an address of nine or ten thousand hands to stand by this Parliament, when it was only told them that it was a petition against hackney-coaches; and that to-day they had put out another, to undeceive the world and to clear themselves. After I had received the money we went homewards; but over against Somerset House, hearing the noise of guns, we landed, and found the Strand full of soldiers. So I took up my money and went to Mrs. Johnson, my Lord's sempstress, and giving her my money to lay up, Doling and I went up stairs to a window, and looked out and saw the Foot face the Horse and beat them back, and stood bawling and calling in the street for a free Parliament and money. By and by a drum was heard to beat a march, coming towards them, and they all got ready again and faced them, and they proved to be of the same mind with them; and so they made a great deal of joy to see one another. After all this, I went home on foot, to lay up my money, and change my stockings and shoes. I this day left off my great skirt suit, and put on my white suit, with silver lace coat,[1] and went over to Harper's, where I met with W. Simonds, Doling, Luellin, and three merchants, one of which had occasion to use a porter, and so they sent for one, and James the soldier came, who told us how they had been all day and night upon their guard at St. James's, and that through the whole town they did resolve to stand to what they had begun, and that to-mor-

---

[1] Pepys' father was a tailor, whence, perhaps, the importance he attaches throughout the Diary to dress; it is evidently more than vanity.

row he did believe they would go into the city, and be received there. After this we went to a sport called, selling of a horse for a dish of eggs and herrings, and sat talking there till almost twelve at night.

3rd. Drank my morning draft at Harper's, and was told there that the soldiers were all quiet upon promise of pay. Thence to St. James's Park, back to Whitehall, where, in a guard chamber, I saw about thirty or forty 'prentices of the city, who were taken at twelve o'clock last night, and brought prisoners hither. Thence to my office, where I paid a little more money to some of the soldiers under Lieut. Col. Miller, (who held out the tower against the Parliament, after it was taken away from Fitch by the Committee of Safety, and yet he continued in his office.) About noon Mrs. Turner [1] came to speak with me and Joyce, and I took them and showed them the manner of the Houses sitting, the doorkeeper very civilly opening the door for us. We went walking all over White Hall, whither General Monk was newly come, and we saw all his forces march by in

---

[1] Jane, daughter of John Pepys of Norfolk, married to John Turner, sergeant-at-law; their only child, Theophila, is frequently mentioned as The or Theoph.

very good plight, and stout officers. After dinner I went to hear news, but only found that the Parliament House was most of them with Monk at White Hall, and that in passing through the town he had many calls to him for a free Parliament, but little other welcome. I saw, in the Palace Yard, how unwilling some of the old soldiers were yet to go out of town without their money, and swore if they had it not in three days, as they were promised, they would do them more mischief in the country than if they had stayed here ; and that is very likely, the country being all discontented. The town and guards are already full of Monk's soldiers. It growing dark, to take a turn in the Park, where Theoph (she was sent for to us to dinner) outran my wife and another poor woman, that laid a pot of ale with me that she would outrun her."

To a modern reader such diversions may appear questionable for a respectable female to engage in ; but they will recollect it was a simple frolic after dark, in Hyde Park, and not to be paralleled by what is now an every-day occurrence, viz., to witness females pick up a given amount of eggs, pebbles, or potatoes, in a given time, and for a stated consideration in good current dollars. Within a few years we have wit-

nessed one of these " swift Camillas scour the
plain " — for some hours — pantalooned and
high kilted, and having successfully achieved
her task, she nonchalantly bowed to the de-
lighted public and retired to private life as cool
as a cucumber, and fresh as a daisy.   On the
day previous, we are also informed that Pepys
himself, and a party of merchant friends, met
at Harper's tavern, and there disported themselves with an amusement called " selling of a
horse for a dish of eggs and herrings ; " but as a
per contra to this plebeian funning, we have a
recent instance of a batch of half-fuddled New
York Aldermen indulging in a regular set to at
hop scotch and leap frog, after the onerous labors
of the supper-table were over, while an assem-
blage of Councilmen found entertainment the
other day, in throwing inkstands at each other's
heads.   To this illustration of the text, we may
overtly mention the case of a distinguished English duke, of the ancient and honorable house of
Beaufort, who only a few years ago was fined
one hundred pounds for an assault on a peaceable, private citizen, who was simply looking at
said Duke unbending his noble mind by playing
at the elegant amusement of " Aunt Sally."
Mais chacun à son goût ; or, as the old Scotch

woman said when she kissed her cow — " Every ane to their fancy."

" 4*th*. All the news to-day is, that the Parliament this morning voted the House to be made up four hundred forthwith. Discourse at an alehouse about Marriott, the great eater, so I was ashamed to eat what I could have done. I met Spicer in Lincoln's Inn Court, buying of a hanging-jack to roast birds upon. My wife killed her turkeys that came out of Zealand with my Lord, and could not get her maid Jane to kill any thing at any time.

5*th*. (Lord's Day.) At church I saw Dick Cumberland, newly come out of the country from his living. In the Court of Wards I saw the three Lords Commissioners sitting upon some action where Mr. Scobell was concerned, and my Lord Fountaine took him up very roughly about some things that he said.

6*th*. To Westminster, where we found the soldiers, all set in the Palace Yard, to make way for General Monk to come to the House. I stood upon the steps and saw Monk go by, he making observance to the judges as he went along.

7*th*. Went to Vaul's school, where he that made the speech for the seventh form in praise

of the Founder, did show a book which Mr.
Crumlum had lately got, which he believed to
be of the Founder's own writing. My brother
John came off as well as any of the rest in the
speeches. To the Hall, where in the Palace I
saw Monk's soldiers abuse Billing, and all the
Quakers, that were at a meeting-place there,
and indeed the soldiers did use them very
roughly, and were to blame. This day Mr.
Crewe told me that my Lord St. John is for a
free Parliament, and that he is very great with
Monk, who hath now the absolute command
and power to do anything that he hath a mind
to do.

9*th*. Before I was out of my bed I heard the
soldiers very busy in the morning, getting their
horses ready when they lay at Hilton's, but I
knew not their meaning in so doing. In the
Hall I understand how Monk is this morning
gone into London with his army; and Mr.
Fage told me that he do believe that Monk is
gone to secure some of the Common Council
of the city, who were very high yesterday there,
and did vote that they would not pay any taxes
till the House was filled up. I went to my
office, where I wrote to my Lord after I had
been at the Upper Bench, where Sir Robert

Pye this morning came to desire his discharge from the Tower, but it could not be granted. I called at Mr. Harper's, who told me how Monk had this day clapt up many of the Common Council, and that the Parliament had voted that he should pull down their gates and portcullises, their posts and their chains, which he do intend to do, and do lie in the city all night. To Westminster Hall, where I heard an action very finely pleaded between my Lord Dorset and some other noble persons, his lady and other ladies of quality being there, and it was about £330 per annum, which was to be paid to a poor Spittal, which was given by some of his predecessors, and given on his side.

10*th.* Mr. Fage told me what Monk had done in the city, how he had pulled down the most part of the gates and chains that they could break down, and that he was now gone back to White Hall. The city look mighty blank and cannot tell what in the world to do; the Parliament having this day ordered that the Common Council sit no more, but that new ones be chosen, according to what qualifications they shall give them.

11*th.* I heard the news of a letter from Monk, who was now gone into the city again,

and did resolve to stand for the sudden filling
up of the House, and it was very strange how
the countenance of men in the Hall was all
changed with joy in half an hour's time.   So I
went to the lobby, where I saw the Speaker
reading of the letter, and after it was read, Sir
A. Haselrigge came out very angry, and Billing,
standing at the door, took him by the arm and
cried, 'Thou man, will thy beast carry thee no
longer? thou must fall!'   We took coach for
the city to Guildhall, where the Hall was full
of people expecting Monk and the Lord Mayor
to come thither, and all very joyful.   Met
Monk coming out of the chamber where he
had been with the mayor and alderman, but
such a shout I never heard in all my life, crying out, 'God bless your Excellence!'   Here
I met with Mr. Lock,[1] and took him to an alehouse ; when we were come together, he told
us the substance of the letter that went from
Mark to the Parliament; wherein, after com-
plaints that he and his officers were put upon
such offices against the city as they could not
do with any content or honor, it states, that
there are many members now in the House

---

[1] Matthew Locke, the celebrated composer.

that were of the late Tyrannical Committee of Safety. That Lambert and Vane are now in town, contrary to the vote of Parliament. That many of the House do press for new oaths to be put upon men; whereas we have more cause to be sorry for the many oaths that we have already taken and broken. That the late petition of the fanatique people presented by Barebones,[1] for the imposing of an oath upon all sorts of people, was received by the House with thanks. That therefore he did desire that all writs for filling up of the House be issued by Friday next, and that in the meantime he would retire into the city, and only leave them guards for the security of the House and Council. The occasion of this was the order that he had last night to go into the city and disarm them and take away their charter; whereby he and his officers said that the House had a mind to put them upon things that should make them odious; and so it would be in their power to do what they would with them. We were told that the Parliament had sent Scott[2] and Robin-

[1] Praise God Barebones, an active member of the Parliament called by his name. He appeared at the head of a band of fanatics, and alarmed Monk, who well knew his influence. He was a leather-seller in Fleet Street, London.

[2] Thomas Scott, recently made Secretary of State, had

son to Monk this afternoon, but he would not hear them; and that the Mayor and Aldermen had offered their own houses for himself and his officers; and that his soldiers would lack for nothing.   And indeed I saw many people give the soldiers drink and money, and all along the streets cried, 'God bless them!' and extraordinary good words.   Hence we went to a merchant's house hard by, where I saw Sir Nich. Crisp,[1] and so we went to the Star tavern (Monk being at Benson's).   In Cheapside there was a great many bonfires, and Bow bells and all the bells in all the churches as we went home were a ringing.   Hence we went homewards, it being about ten at night.   But the

---

signed the king's death-warrant, for which he was executed at Charing Cross, 16th October, 1660.   He and Luke Robinson were both members of Parliament and of the Council of State, and selected, as firm adherents to the Rump, to watch Monk's proceedings; and never was a mission more signally unsuccessful.   Scott, before his execution, desired to have it written on his tombstone, "Thomas Scott, who adjudged to death the late king."

[1] An eminent merchant, and one of the farmers of the customs.   He had advanced large sums to assist Charles I., who created him a baronet.   He died 26th February, 1665, aged sixty-seven, and was buried in the church of St. Mildred, Bread Street.   For an account of him and his magnificent house at Hammersmith, on the site of which Brandenburgh House was built, see Lyon's Environs and other local histories.

common joy, that was everywhere to be seen! The number of bonfires, there being fourteen between St. Dunstan's and Temple Bar, and at Strand Bridge,[1] I could at one time tell thirty-one fires. In King Street seven or eight; and all along, burning, and roasting, and drinking for rumps. There being rumps tied upon sticks and carried up and down. The butchers at the May Pole in the Strand[2] rang a peal with their knives when they were going to sacrifice their rump. On Ludgate Hill there was one turning of the spit that had a rump tied upon it, and another basting of it. Indeed it was past imagination, both the greatness and the sudness of it. At one end of the street you would think there was a whole lane of fire, and so hot that we were fain to keep on the further side."

12*th*. (Lord's Day.) In the morning, it being Lord's Day, to White Hall, where Dr. Holmes preached; but I staid not to hear, but walking in the court, I heard that Sir Arthur Hasel-rigge was newly gone into the city to Monk,

---

[1] Described in Maitland's History of London as a handsome bridge crossing the Strand, near the east end of Catherine Street, under which a small stream glided from the fields into the Thames, near Somerset House.

[2] Where stands the church of St. Mary-le-Strand.

and that Monk's wife [1] removed from White Hall last night. After dinner, I heard that Monk had been at Paul's in the morning, and the people had shouted much at his coming out of the church. In the afternoon he was at a church in Broad Street, whereabout he do lodge. Walking with Mr. Kirton's [2] apprentice during evening church, and looking for a tavern to drink at, but not finding any open, we durst not knock. To my father's, where Charles Glascocke was overjoyed to see how things are now; who told me the boys had last night broke Barebones' windows.

13th. This day Monk was invited to White Hall to dinner by my Lords; not seeming willing, he would not come. I went to Mr. Fage from my father's, who had been this afternoon with Monk, who did promise to live and die with the city, and for the honor of the city; and indeed the city is very open-handed to the soldiers, that they are most of

---

[1] Anne Clarges, daughter of a blacksmith, and bred a milliner; mistress, and afterwards wife, of General Monk, over whom she exercised the greatest influence.

[2] Thomas Kirton was a bookseller in St. Paul's Churchyard, at the sign of "The King's Arms." His death in October, 1667, is recorded in Smith's Obituary, printed for the Camden Society.

them drunk all day, and had money given them.

14*th*. My wife, hearing Mr. Moore's voice in my dressing-chamber, got herself ready, and came down, and challenged him for her valentine. To Westminster Hall, there being many new remonstrances and declarations from many counties to Monk and the city, and one coming from the North from Sir Thomas Fairfax.[1] I heard that the Parliament had now changed the oath so much talked of to a promise; and that, among other qualifications for the members that are to be chosen, one is that no man, nor the son of any man, that hath been in arms during the life of the father, shall be capable of being chosen to sit in Parliament. This day, by an order of the House, Sir H. Vane[2] was sent out of town to his house in Lincoln-shire.

15*th*. No news to-day, but all quiet to see what the Parliament will do about the issuing

[1] Thomas Lord Fairfax, mentioned before. He had succeeded to the Scotch Barony of Fairfax, of Cameron, on the death of his father in 1647; even after his accession to the title, he is frequently styled "Sir Thomas" in the pamphlets and papers of the day.

[2] Sir H. Vane had married Frances, daughter of Sir Christopher Wray, of Ashby, Lincolnshire, Bart.

of the writs to-morrow for the filling up of the House, according to Monk's desire.

17th. To Westminster Hall, where I heard that some of the members of the House were gone to meet some of the secluded members and General Monk in the city. Thence to White Hall, thinking to hear more news, where I met Mr. Hunt, who told me how Monk had sent for all his goods that he had here, into the city; and yet again he told me, that some of the members of the House had this day laid in firing into their lodgings at Whitehall for a good while, so that we are at a great stand to think what will become of things, whether Monk will stand by the Parliament or no. Drank with Mr. Wotten, who told me a great many stories of comedies that he had formerly seen acted, and the names of the principal actors, and gave me a very good account of it."

In glancing at the history of this period, one remarkable feature in the aspect of the times is the uncertain and doubtful issue of the passing events of the day. The Cavaliers seemed to be gathering new life and animation for the coming struggle, in which they had everything to gain, and little to lose, being already over-fleeced by the fines and other penal exactions of the Commonwealth ; while the adherents of the latter were stirring heaven and earth to place Monk or Richard Cromwell in the Protectorate. The army, always the main stay and bulwark of the Commonwealth, was to a man against the king, while Monk, like a wary and skilful gambler, was deeply intent in studying the cards that chance had dealt out to him. He required, however, short space for deliberation, for the English nation, tired of the multitude of its masters, was again ready to put its neck into the yoke of *one ;* and the following interesting passages of the Diary inform us how the denouement of this grand drama was introduced. Pepys, with his father and his brother John, had gone to Magdalen College, Cambridge, to procure a certificate for the entrance of the latter, and on his setting out to return home we have the following details : —

" 27*th*. Up by four o'clock ; Mr. Blayton and I took horse and straight to Safforn Walden, where, at the White Hart, we set up our horses, and took the master of the house to show us Audley End House,[1] who took us on foot through

[1] Then the residence of James Howard, third Earl of Suffolk. It was built by Thomas, the first Earl, at the commence-

the park, and to the house, where the housekeeper showed us all through the house, in
which the stateliness of the ceilings, chimney-
pieces, and form of the whole was exceedingly
worth seeing.　He took us into the cellar, where
we drank most admirable drink, a health to the
king.　Here I played on my flageolette, there
being an excellent echo.　He showed us excellent pictures ; two especially, those of the four
Evangelists and Henry VIII.　In our going my
landlord carried us through a very old hospital
or almshouse, where forty poor people were
maintained ; a very old foundation ; and over
the chimney-piece was an inscription in brass :
" Orate pro anima Thomæ Bird," [1] &c.[2]　They
brought me a draught of their drink in a brown
bowl tipt with silver, which I drank off, and in
the bottom was a picture of the Virgin with the
child in her arms, done in silver.　So we took
leave, the road pretty good, but the weather
raining, to Epping.

ment of the seventeenth century, and called after his maternal
ancestor, Lord Chancellor Audley, to whom the monastery of
Wa'den, the site of which is occupied by the present house,
had been granted at the Dissolution.

[1] Byrd in the original.

[2] The inscription and the bowl are still to be seen in the
almshouse.

28*th*. Up in the morning, and had some red herrings to our breakfast, while my boot-heel was a-mending, by the same token the boy left the hole as big as it was before. Then to horse for London, through the forest, where we found the way good, but only in one path, which we kept as if we had rode through a kennel all the way. We found the shops all shut, and the militia of the red regiment in arms at the old Exchange, among whom I found and spoke to Nich. Osborne, who told me that it was a thanksgiving-day through the city for the return of the Parliament. At Paul's I light, Mr. Blayton holding my horse, where I found Dr. Reynolds[1] in the pulpit, and General Monk there, who was to have a great entertainment at Grocers' Hall. I found my Lord at dinner glad to see me.

29*th*. To my office. Mr. Moore told me how my Lord is chosen General at sea by the Council, and that it is thought that Monk will be joined with him therein. This day my Lord came to the House, the first time since he came to town; but he had been at the Council before. My cousin Morton gave me a brave cup of metheglin, the first I ever drank.

1 Edward Reynolds, **D. D.,** Dean of Christ Church, and afterwards Bishop of Norwich. He died 1676: his works are well **known.**

March 1*st.* Out of the box where my Lord's pamphlets lay, I chose as many as I had a mind to have for my own use, and left the rest. I went to Mr. Crewe's, whither Mr. Thomas was newly come to town, being sent with Sir H. Yelverton,[1] my old schoolfellow at Paul's School, to bring the thanks of the country to General Monk for the return of the Parliament.

2*nd.* I went early to my Lord at Mr. Crewe's, where I spoke to him. Here were a great many come to see him, as Secretary Thurloe,[2] who is now by the Parliament chosen again Secretary of State. To Westminster Hall, where I saw Sir G. Booth at liberty. This day I hear the City militia is put into good posture, and it is thought that Monk will not be able to do any great matter against them now, if he had a mind. I understand that my Lord Lambert did yesterday send a letter to the Council, and that to-night he is to come and appear to the Council

[1] Son of Sir Christopher Yelverton, the first Baronet. Grandson of Sir Henry Yelverton, Judge C. P., author of the Reports. He married Susan, Baroness Grey de Ruthyn, which title descended to his issue. His son was afterwards advanced to the dignity of Viscount Longueville, and his grandson to the Earldom of Sussex.

[2] John Thurloe, who had been Secretary of State to the two Protectors, but was never employed after the Restoration, though the King solicited his services. Ob. 1668.

iu persou. Sir Arthur Haselrigge do not yet appear in the House. Great is the talk of a single person, and that it would now be Charles, George, or Richard again,[1] for the last of which my Lord St. John[2] is said to speak high. Great also is the dispute now in the House, in whose name the writs shall run for the next Parliament; and it is said that Mr. Prin, in open house, said, ' In King Charles's.'

3rd. To Westminster Hall, where I found that my Lord was last night voted one of the Generals at sea, and Monk the other. I met my Lord in the Hall, who bid me come to him at noon. After dinner, I to Warwick House,[3] in Holborne, to my Lord, where he dined with my Lord of Manchester,[4] Sir Dudley North,[5] my Lord Fiennes,[6] and my Lord Barkly.[7] I

[1] Charles Stuart; George Monk; Richard Cromwell.

[2] Oliver St. John; see Feb. 7, 1659-60.

[3] Near Gray's Inn, where Warwick Court now stands.

[4] The Parliamentary General, afterwards particularly instrumental in the King's Restoration, became Chamberlain of the Household, K. G., a privy Counsellor, and Chancellor of the University of Cambridge. He died in 1671, having been five times married.

[5] Sir Dudley North, K. B., became the fourth Lord North on the death of his father, in 1666. Ob. 1677.

[6] John, third son of William, first Viscount Say and Sele, and one of Oliver's Lords.

[7] George, thirteenth Lord Berkeley of Berkeley, created Earl of Berkeley 1679. There were at this time two Lord Berkeleys, each possessing a town house called after his name,

stayed in the great hall, talking with some gentlemen there, till they all came out. Then I by
coach with my Lord, to Mr. Crewe's, in our
way talking of public things. He told me he
feared there was new design hatching, as if
Monk had a mind to get into the saddle. Returning, met with Mr. Gifford, who told me, as
I hear from many, that things are in a doubtful
posture, some of the Parliament being willing
to keep the power in their hands. After I had
left him, I met Tom Harper; he talked huge
high that my Lord Protector would come in
place again, which indeed is much talked of
again, though I do not see it possible.

5*th*. To Westminster by water, only seeing
Mr. Pinkny [1] at his own house, where he showed

which misled Pennant and other biographers following in his
track. George, thirteenth Lord Berkeley of Berkeley, advanced to the Earldom in 1679, the Peer here spoken of, lived
at Berkeley House, in the parish of St. John's, Clerkenwell,
which had been in his family for three generations, and had a
country seat at Durdans near Epsom, mentioned by Evelyn
and Pepys. His death took place in 1689. The other nobleman,
originally known as Sir John Berkeley, and in the service of
Charles I., created in 1658 Baron Berkeley of Stratton, subsequently filled many high offices in the State, and was in 1670
Lord Lieutenant of Ireland, and in 1674 went Ambassador to
France, and died in 1678. He built a splendid mansion in Pic-
cadilly, called also Berkeley House, upon the site of which
Devonshire House now stands.

[1] Probably Leonard Pinkney, who was clerk of the Kitchen,
at the ensuing Coronation Feast.

me how he had always kept the Lion and Uni-
corne in the back of his chimney, bright, in expectation of the King's coming again. At home
I found Mr. Hunt, who told me how the Parliament had voted that the Covenant be printed
and hung in churches again. Great hopes of
the King's coming again.

6th. Shrove Tuesday. I called Mr. Shepley, and we both went up to my Lord's lodgings
at Mr. Crewe's, where he bids us go home again,
and get a fire against an hour after, which we
did, at White Hall, whither he came, and after
talking with him about our going to sea, he
called me by myself into the garden, where he
asked me how things went with me. He bid
me look out now at this good turn some place,
and he would use all his own, and all the interest of the friends that he had in England, to do
me good ; and asked me whether I could, without too much inconvenience, go to sea as his
secretary, and bid me think of it. He also began to talk of things of State, and he told me
that he should want one in that capacity at sea,
that he might trust in, and therefore he would
have me to go. He told me also, that he did
believe the King would come in, and did discourse with me about it, and about the affection

of the people and city, at which I was full glad.
Mr. Hawley brought me a seaman that had
promised 10l. to him if he got him a purser's place, which I think to endeavor to do.
My uncle Tom inquires about the Knights of
Windsor, of which he desires to be one.   To
see Mrs. Jem, at whose chamber door I found
a couple of ladies, but she not being there, we
hunted her out, and found that she and another
had hid themselves behind a door.   Well, they
all went down into the dining-room, where it
was full of tag, rag, and bob-tail, dancing, singing, and drinking, of which I was ashamed, and
after I had staid a dance or two, I went away.
Wrote by the post, by my Lord's command, for
P. Goods to come up presently; for my Lord
intends to go forth with goods to the Swiftsure
till the Nazeby be ready.   This day I hear that
the Lords do intend to sit, a great store of them
are now in town, and, I see, in the Hall to-day.
Overton [1] at Hull do stand out, but can, it is
thought, do nothing; and Lawson, it is said, is
gone with some ships thither, but all that is
nothing.   My Lord told me that there was great
endeavors to bring in the Protector again; but
he told me, too, that he did not believe it would

___
[1] The Parliamentary General.

last long if he were brought in ; no, nor the King neither, (though he seems to think that he will come in) unless he carry himself very soberly and well. Everybody now drinks the King's health without any fear, whereas before it was very private that a man dare do it. Monk, this day, is feasted at Mercer's Hall, and is invited, one after another, to the twelve Halls in London. Many think that he is honest yet, and some or more think him to be a fool, that would raise himself, but think that he will undo himself by endeavoring it.

7th (Ash Wednesday). Washington told me, upon my question, whether he knew of any place now ready, that I might have by power over my friends, that this day Mr. G. Montagu[1] was to be made Custos Rotulorum for Westminster, and that I might get to be named by him Clerk of the Peace ; but my Lord he believes Mr. Montagu had already promised it, and that it was given him only that he might gratify one person with the place I look for. Going homeward, my Lord overtook me in his coach, and called me in, and so I went with

[1] George Montagu, fifth son of Henry, first Earl of Manchester, afterwards M. P. for Dover, and father of the first Earl of Halifax.

him to St. James, and G. Montagu being gone
to White Hall, we walked over the Park thither,
all the way he discoursing of the times, and of
the change of things since last year, and won-
dering how he could bear with so great disap-
pointment as he did. He did give me the best
advice that he could what was best for me,
whether to stay or go with him, and offered all
the ways that could be, how he would do me
good, with the greatest liberty and love that
could be. This day, according to order, Sir
Arthur[1] appeared at the house; what was done
I know not, but there was all the Rumpers almost come to the house to-day. My Lord did
seem to wonder much why Lambert was so
willing to be put into the Tower, and thinks he
has some design in it; but I think he is so poor
he cannot use his liberty for debts, if he were
at liberty; and so it is as good and better for
him to be there than anywhere else. My father
left my uncle with his leg very dangerous, and
do not believe he can continue long. My uncle
did acquaint him that he did intend to make
me his heir, and give my brother Tom something, (and to leave) something to raise por-

---

[1] Sir Arthur Hasselrigge.

tions for John and Pall.[1] I pray God he may be as good as his word. This news and my Lord's great kindness makes me very cheerful within.

8th. To Westminster Hall, where there was a general damp over men's minds and faces upon some of the officers of the army being about making a remonstrance upon Charles Stuart or any single person ; but at noon it was told that the general had put a stop to it, so all was well again. Here I met with Jasper, who was to bring me to my Lord at the lobby; whither sending a note to my Lord, he comes out to me and gives me directions to look after getting some money for him from the Admiralty, seeing that things are so unsafe, that he would not lay out a farthing for the State till he had received some money of theirs. This afternoon, some of the officers of the army, and some of the Parliament, had a conference at White Hall, to make all right again, but I know not what was done. At the Dog[2] Tavern, Captain Phillip Holland, with whom I advised

---

[1] John and Paulina Pepys, our author's brother and sister.
[2] A house still existing in Holywell Street, in the Strand, bears this name, but from mention elsewhere, the Dog Tavern here recorded must have been in Westminster.

how to make some advantage of my Lord's going to sea, told me to have five or six servants
entered on board as dead men, and I to give
them what wages I pleased, and so their pay
to be mine; he also urged me to take the Secretary's place that my **Lord** did proffer me.
Then in comes Mr. Wade and **Mr.** Sterry, Secretary to the Plenipotentiary in Denmark, who
brought the news of the death of the King of
Sweden,[1] at Gottenburgh, the 3d of last month,
and he told me what a great change he found
when he came here, the secluded members being restored.

9th. To my Lord at his lodging, and came
to Westminster with him in the coach; and
Mr. Budley and he in the Painted Chamber
walked a good while; and I telling him that I
was willing and ready to go with him to sea,
he agreed that I should, and advised me what
to write to Mr. Downing about it. This day it
was resolved that the writs **do** go out in the
name of the Keepers of the Liberty, and I hear
that it is resolved privately that a treaty be
offered with the King; and that Monk did
check his soldiers highly for what they did yesterday.

[1] Charles Gustavus.

10*th*. To my father in his cutting house, and told him my resolution to go to sea with my Lord, and we resolved of letting my wife be at Mr. Bowyer's.[1]

12*th*. Rode to Huntsmore to Mr. Bowyer's, where I found him and all well, and willing to have my wife come and board with them while I was at sea. Here I lay and took a spoonful of honey and a nutmeg, scraped for my cold by Mr. Bowyer's direction."

The following entry indicates the doubtful position of affairs, and the sentiments of the army with regard to a monarchy : —

" 13*th*. At my Lord's lodging, who told me that I was to be Secretary, and Crewe deputy treasurer to the Fleet, at which I was troubled, but I could not help it. This day the Parliament voted all that had been by the former Rump against the House of Lords to be void, and that to-night the writs go out without any qualification. Things seem very doubtful what will be the end of all ; for the Parliament seems to be strong for the King, while the soldiers do all talk against."

Yes, they all talked against the restoration of Charles, but the man who could have resolved

---

[1] Bowyer had probably married Mrs. Pepys's mother.

their *talk* into action was slumbering in Westminster Abbey; and while their hostility to the
coming man evaporated in frothy threats and
pointless vituperation, the heads to conceive
and the hands to execute were quietly trans-
ferring the allegiance of army and navy — Re-
publican and Royalist — to their legitimate
sovereign, Charles Stuart. On the following
day, Pepys has this entry: " This day I saw
General Monk, and methought he seemed a
dull, heavy man." Ah Samuel, Samuel Pepys!
every day's experience proves the fallacy
of judging men by their *seeming*. How often
do *seeming* saints, apparently ripe for transla-
tion to better society above, turn out very devils
disguised in humanity! How often does the
seeming patriot solemnly protest and swear to
his honest devotion to his constituents' interests
with the bribe and purchase money for his vote
in his breeches pocket! And how often do we
find, in the records of eminent men, the most
marked contrast between their real greatness and
their outward seeming! As the old poet tells us,

> " appearances deceive,
> And this one maxim is a standing rule —
> Men are not what they seem."

To Samuel Pepys, his namesake, Samuel

Johnson, would inevitably have " seemed a dull, heavy man." So would Oliver Goldsmith, Edmund Burke, Thomas Chalmers, John Foster, and Robert Hall.

As for Sir Walter Scott, what would have been our diarist's conclusion had he looked upon those lustreless, dreamy eyes, seeming to gaze on vacancy from under those shaggy, pent-house eyebrows as he sat at the Clerk's table in the Court of Session, perhaps evolving those matchless creations of an exuberant and glowing imagination which in all after times were to delight and instruct an admiring world? Utterly unconscious of the myriads of eyes gazing upon him as they would have gazed on a magnificent old lion through the bars of an iron cage, there he sat day by day, that miraculous pen ever in motion. Yet world-wide as his fame was, there were about him no airs of greatness, no attempt at acting. In simple, quiet, manly dignity, he appeared to sit like the Mysterious Sphinx, looking into a world of shadowy unrealities, as if calling up before him those wonderful, yet life-like creatures that fill his more wonderful and life-like dramas ; and amid all this, the utter unpretending simplicity of the man was as delightful as the high character and renown of the author. This fully justifies the remark of the Forfarshire farmer, who, on having Scott pointed out to him as he sat in his accustomed place in the Court of Session, exclaimed, " What! that sleepy-looking carle wi' the white hair, at the north side o' the table — that Sir Walter! it's no possible! Od, he looks juist like ane o' our farmer-folk, in the Carse o' Gowrie, in his Sunday gear! Hoo I wish I could shake hands and tak' a snuff wi' him! but as that seems no juist convenient, there's nae harm in saying, God bless Sir Walter Scott! "

But to return to Monk. Cromwell, a much more profound judge of character than Pepys, formed a high estimate of the military talents of Monk, made him his lieutenant-general, and gave him the chief command in Scotland. But the sagacious usurper had strong suspicions of Monk's sincerity, and not long before his death, wrote him a letter, to which he added this postscript: " There be that tell me that there is a certain cunning fellow in Scotland, called George Monk, who is said to lie in wait there to introduce Charles Stuart. I pray you use your diligence to apprehend him, and send him up to me." It will thus be obvious that Monk's fire and alacrity of spirit were more of an inward flame, and burned on an unseen and immaterial altar, and that the outward manifestation of unwieldy inertness with which he was chargeable was but the rude grandeur of the embrasured rock which only awakes from its slumber at the fierce blare of the trumpet-call to battle.

Having received the thanks of the House for his public services, Monk, in his reply, adverted to the numerous applications he had received for a full and free Parliament, at the same time expressing his dislike of oaths and engagements, and his hopes that neither Fanatic nor Cavalier would again be intrusted with civil or military power. By some his speech was thought arrogant and dictatorial. "The servant," said Scott, " has already learned to give directions to his masters." It was no marvel Monk should direct his masters, for, ere this date, he had been bargained for and bought by another master, who could offer a heavier bribe with an earldom for the bait, and while he appeared the prompt and humble servant of the Common Council, he was maturing a deep scheme of masterly policy for the total overthrow of the Commonwealth, and the return of the exiled monarch to the throne of his fathers.

5

"14*th.* To my Lord's, where infinity of applications to him and to me. To my great trouble, my Lord gives me all the papers that was
given to him, to put in order and to give him
an account of them. Here I got half a piece
of a person of Mr. Wright's recommending to
my Lord, to be Chaplain of the Speaker frigate.
I went hence to St. James, to speak with Mr.
Clerke,[1] Monk's Secretary, about getting some
soldiers removed out of Huntington to Oundle,
which my Lord told me he did to do a courtesy
to the town, that he might have the greater
interest in them, in the choice of the next Parliament ; and that he intends to be chosen himself, but that he might have Mr. G. Montagu
and my Lord Mandeville,[2] chose there in spite
of the Bernards. This done, I saw General
Monk, and methought he seemed a dull heavy
heavy man. I did promise to give my wife all
that I have in the world, but my books, in case
I should die at sea. After supper I went to
Westminster Hall, and the Parliament sat till
ten at night, thinking and being expected to
dissolve themselves to-day, but they did not.

[1] Clement Clerke, of Lawnde Abbey, Leicester County, created a baronet in 1661.

[2] Eldest son of the Earl of Manchester.

Great talk to-night that the discontented officers, did think this night to make a stir, but
were prevented.

15*th*. Early packing my things to be sent by
cart with the rest of my Lord's. At Well's I
met Tom Alcock, one that went to school with
me at Huntingdon, but I had not seen him
these sixteen years.

16*th*. To Westminster, where I heard how
the Parliament had this day dissolved themselves, and did pass very cheerfully through the
Hall, and the speaker without his mace. The
whole Hall was joyful thereat, as well as themselves, and now they begin to talk loud of the
King. To-night I am told, that yesterday about
five o'clock in the afternoon, one came with a
ladder to the Great[1] Exchange, and wiped
with a brush the great inscription that was on
King Charles, and that there was a great bonfire made in the Exchange, and people called
out, 'God bless King Charles the Second."[2]

[1] So called during the Commonwealth, in lieu of Royal.

[2] "Then the writing in golden letters, that was engraven
under the statue of Charles I. in the Royal Exchange (Exit
tyrannus, Regum ultimus, anno libertatis Angliæ, Anno
Domini 1648, Januarie xxx), was washed out by a painter,
who, in the daytime, raised a ladder, and with a pot and
brush, washed the writing quite out, threw down his pot and
brush, and said it should never do him any more service, in

Between the date of our last extract and the
middle of May, great changes had taken place
in the feelings and opinions of the people of
England, extending more or less among all
classes — Whigs, Tories, Puritans, Indepen-
dents, *et id genus omne;* and as will be seen by
the following passages from the Secretary's
Diary, an expedition which he accompanied,
had put to sea, and was now about to bring the
son of the beheaded monarch back " to his ain
again." It will be observed that the pecuniary
distress of the royal family then residing in Holland was, at the moment of the Restoration,
very great. The king's clothes, says the fastid-
ious son of the defunct London tailor, " not
being worth forty shillings." Andrew Mar-
vell, alluding to the poor condition for clothes
and money in which Charles Stuart was at this
time, observes, —

"At length, by wonderful impulse of fate,
The people call him back to help the state;
And what is more, they send him money, too,
And clothe him all from head to foot anew."

regard that it had the honor to put out rebels' hand-writing.
He then came down, took away his ladder, not a misword said
to him, and by whose order it was done was not then known.
The merchants were glad and joyful; many people were
gathered together, and against the Exchange made a bonfire." — *Rugge's Diurnal.*

" *May* 14*th*. In the morning the Hague was clearly to be seen by us. My Lord went up in his night-gown into the cuddy, to see how to dispose thereof for himself and us that belong to him, to give order for our removal to-day. Some nasty Dutchmen came on board to proffer their boats to carry things from us on shore, &c., to get money by us. Before noon some gentlemen came on board from the shore to kiss my Lord's hands. And by and by Mr. North and Dr. Clerke went to kiss the Queen of Bohemia's [1] hands, from my Lord, with twelve attendants from on board to wait on them, among which I sent my boy,[2] who, like myself, is with child to see any strange thing. After noon they came back again, after having kissed the Queen of Bohemia's hand, and were sent again by my Lord to do the same to the Prince of Orange.[3] So I got the Captain to ask leave for me to go, which my Lord did give, and I, taking my boy and Judge Advocate with me, went in company with them. The weather bad ; we were sadly washed when we come near the shore, it being very hard to land there. The shore is so, all

---

[1] Daughter of James the First.
[2] Young Edward Montagu, afterwards styled " the child."
[3] Afterwards William the Third.

the country between that and the Hague, all
sand. The rest of the company got a coach by
themselves; Mr. Creed and I went in the fore
part of a coach, wherein were two very pretty
ladies, very fashionable, and with black patches,
who very merrily sang all the way, and that
very well, and were very free to kiss two blades
that were with them. The Hague is a most
neat place in all respects. The houses so neat
in all places and things as is possible. Here
we walked up and down a great while, the town
. being now very full of Englishmen, for that the
Londoners were come on shore to-day. But
going to see the Prince,[1] he was gone forth with
his governor, and so we walked up and down
the town and court to see the place; and by the
help of a stranger, an Englishman, we saw a
great many places, and were made to understand many things, as the intention of may-
poles, which we saw there standing at every
great man's door, of different greatness according to the quality of the person. About ten at
night the Prince comes home, and we found an
easy admission. His attendance very inconsiderable as for a Prince; but yet handsome, and

[1] Henry, Duke of Gloucester, Charles the Second's youngest
brother.

his tutor a fine man, and himself a very pretty boy. This done, we went to a place we had taken to sup in, where a sallet and two or three bones of mutton were provided for a matter of ten of us, which was very strange. The Judge and I lay in one press bed, there being two more in the same room; my boy sleeping on a bench by me.

15*th.* We lay till past three o'clock, then up and down the town, to see it by daylight; where we saw the soldiers of the Prince's guard, all very fine, and the burghers of the town with their muskets as bright as silver. A schoolmaster, that spoke good English and French, showed us the whole town, and indeed I cannot speak enough of the gallantry of the town. Every body of fashion speaks French or Latin, or both. The women many of them very pretty and in good habits, fashionable, and black spots. We bought a couple of baskets for Mrs. Pierce and my wife. The Judge and I to the Grande Salle, where the States sit in council. The hall is a great place, where the flags that they take from their enemies are all hung up; and things to be sold, as in Westminster Hall, and not much unlike it, but that not so big. To a bookseller's, and bought for the love of the binding three books; the French Psalms, in four parts, Bacon's Organon, and Farnab. Rhetor. By coach to Scheveling again, the wind being very high. We saw two boats overset, and the gallants forced to be pulled on shore by the heels, while their trunks, portmanteaus, hats, and feathers, were swimming in the sea. Among others, the ministers that come with the Commissions (Mr. Case among the rest) sadly dripped. Being in haste, I lost my Copenhagen knife. A gentleman going to kiss my Lord's hand, from the Queen of Bohemia, and I hired a Dutch boat for four rix dollars to carry us on board. We were fain to wait a great while before we could get off from the shore, the sea being very foul. The Dutchman would fain have made all pay that come into our boat besides our company, there being many of our ship's company got in, but some of them had no money, having spent all on shore. Coming on board, we found all the Commissioners of the House of Lords at dinner with my Lord, who after dinner went away for shore. Mr. Morland, now Sir Samuel, was here on board, but I do not find that my Lord or anybody did give him any respect, he being looked upon by him and all men as a knave. Among others, he betrayed **Sir Richard Willis** that married Dr. **F. Jones's** daughter, who had paid him 1000*l.* at one time by the Protector's and Secretary Thurloe's order, for intelligence that he sent concerning the King. In the afternoon my Lord called me on purpose to show me his fine clothes which are now come hither, and indeed are very rich as gold and silver can make them, only his sword he and I do not like. In the afternoon my Lord and I walked together in the coach two hours, talking together upon all sorts of discourse : as religion, wherein he is, as I perceive, wholly sceptical, saying, that indeed the Protestants as to the Church of Rome are wholly fanatiques ; he likes uniformity and form of prayer ; about State-business, among other things he told me that his conversion to the King's cause (for I was saying that I wondered from what time the King could look upon him to become his friend) commenced from his being in the Sound, when he found what usage he was likely to have from a Commonwealth. My Lord, the Captain, and I, supped in my Lord's chamber, where I did perceive that he did begin to show me much more respect that ever he did yet. After supper, my Lord sent for me, intending to have me play at cards with him, but

I not knowing cribbage, we fell into discourse
of many things, and the ship rolled so much that
I was not able to stand, and so he bid me go to
bed.

16*th.*   Come in some with visits, among the
rest one from Admiral Opdam,[1] who spoke
Latin well, but not French nor English, whom
my Lord made me to entertain ; he brought
my Lord a tierce of wine and a barrel of butter
as a present.   Commissioner Pett[2] was now
come to take care to get all things ready for the
King on board.   My Lord in his best suit, this
the first day, in expectation to wait upon the
King.   But Mr. Edward Pickering, coming
from the King, brought word that the King
would not put my Lord to the trouble of coming to him ; but that he would come to the
shore to look upon the fleet to-day, which we
expected, and had our guns ready to fire, and
our scarlet waist-cloathes out and silk pendants,

[1] The Dutch Admiral celebrated in Lord Dorset's ballad,
" To all you ladies now at land."

> " Should foggy Opdam chance to know
>   Our sad and dismal story :
> The Dutch would scorn so weak a foe,
>   And quit their fort at Goree.
> For what resistance can they find
>   From men who've left their hearts behind ? "

[2] Naval commissioner at Chatham.

but he did not come. This evening came Mr.
John Pickering on board, like an ass, with his
feathers and new suit that he had made at the
Hague. My Lord very angry for his staying
on shore, bidding me a little before to send for
him, telling me that he was afraid that, for his
father's sake, he might have some mischief done
him, unless he used the General's name. This
afternoon Mr. Edward Pickering told me in
what a sad, poor condition for clothes and
money the King was, and all his attendants,
when he came to him first from my Lord, their
clothes not being worth forty shillings the best
of them. And how overjoyed the King was
when Sir J. Greenville brought him some money ;
so joyful that he called the Princess Royal[1] and
Duke of York to look upon it, as it lay in the
portmanteau, before it was taken out. My
Lord told me, too, that the Duke of York is
made High Admiral of England.

17th. Dr. Clerke came to tell me that he
heard this morning, by some Dutch that are
come on board already to see the ships, that
there was a Portuguese taken yesterday at the

[1] Mary, eldest daughter of Charles I., and widow of the
Prince of Orange, who died 1646-7. She died December,
1660, leaving a son, afterwards King William the Third of
England.

Hague, that had a design to kill the King. But this I heard afterwards was only the mistake upon one being observed to walk with his sword naked, he having lost his scabbard. Before dinner, Mr. Edward Pickering and I, W. Howe, Pim, and my boy, to Scheveling, where we took coach, and so to the Hague, where walking, intending to find one that might show us the King incognito, I met with Captain Whittington (that had formerly brought a letter to my Lord from the Mayor of London), and he did promise me to do it, but first we went and dined at a French house, but paid 10s. for our part of the club. At dinner, in came Dr. Cade, a merry mad parson of the King's. And they two got the child and me (the others not being able to crowd in) to see the King, who kissed the child very affectionately. Then we kissed his, and the Duke of York's, and the Princess Royal's hands. The King seemed to be a very sober man; and a very splendid Court he hath in the number of persons of quality that are about him, English, very rich in habit. From the King to the Lord Chancellor, who did lie bed-rid of the gout; he spoke very merrily to the child and me. After that, going to see the Queen of Bohemia, I met Dr. Fuller, whom

I sent to a tavern with Mr. Edward Pickering, while I and the rest went to see the Queen, who used us very respectfully; her hand we all kissed. She seems a very debonair, but a plain lady. In a coach of a friend of Dr. Cade, we went to see a house of the Princess Dowager's,[1] in a park about a mile from the Hague, where there is one of the most beautiful rooms for pictures in the whole world. She had here one picture upon the top, with these words, dedicating it to the memory of her husband: — ' Incomparabili marito, inconsolabilis vidua.'[2]

18*th.* Very early up, and, hearing that the Duke of York, our Lord High Admiral, would go on board to-day, Mr. Pickering and I took wagon for Scheveling, leaving the child in Mr. Pierce's hands, with directions to keep within doors all day. But the wind being so very high that no boats could get off from shore, we returned to the Hague (having breakfasted with a gentleman of the Duke's and Commissioner Pett, sent on purpose to give notice to my Lord of his coming) ; where I hear that the child is gone to Delfe to see the town : so we took a scout,

---

[1] Mary, daughter of Charles the First.

[2] And yet, like the Ephesian matron, she was said to be married clandestinely.

very much pleased with the manner and conversation of the passengers, where most speak
French ; went after them and met them by the
way.   We got a smith's boy of the town to go
along with us, and he showed us the church
where Van Trump lies entombed with a very
fine monument.   His epitaph is concluded thus :
— 'Tandem Bello Anglico tantum non victor,
certè invictus, vivere et vincere desiit.'   There
is a sea-fight cut in marble, with the smoke, the
best expressed that ever I saw in my life.
From thence to the great church, that stands in
a fine great market place, over against the Stadt
House, and there I saw a stately tomb of an old
Prince of Orange, of marble and brass ; wherein, among other rarities, there are the angels
with their trumpets expressed as it were crying.
Here were very fine organs in both the churches.
It is a most sweet town, with bridges, and a
river in every street.   In every house of entertainment there hangs in every room a poor
man's box, it being their custom to confirm all
bargains by putting something into the box, and
that binds as fast as any thing.   We also saw
the Guest-house, where it was pleasant to see
what neat preparation there is for the poor.
We saw one poor man a-dying there.   We light

by chance of an English house to drink in, where discourse of the town and the thing that hangs up in the Stadt-house like a bushel, which is a sort of punishment for offenders to carry through the streets over his head, which is a great weight. Back by water, where a pretty, sober, Dutch lass sat reading all the way, and I could not fasten any discourse upon her. We met with Commissioner Pett going down to the water side with Major Harley,[1] who is going upon a despatch into England.

19*th*. Up early and went to Scheveling, where I found no getting on board, though the Duke of York sent every day to see whether he could do it or no. By wagon to Lausdune, where the 365 children were born. We saw the hill where they say the house stood wherein the children were born. The basins wherein the male and female children were baptized do stand over a large table that hangs upon a wall, with the whole story of the thing in Dutch and Latin, beginning, " Margarita Herman Comitissa," &c. This thing was done about 200 years ago.[2]

---

[1] Afterwards Colonel Edward Harley, **M. P. and Governor** of Dunkirk.

[2] This **story** has been frequently **printed.**

20*th*.   (Lord's Day.)   Commissioner Pett at
last came to our lodging, and caused the boats
to go off; so some in one boat and some in
another, we all bid adieu to the shore.   But
through the badness of weather we were in great
danger, and a great while before we could get
to the ship.   This hath not been known four
days together such weather this time of year, a
great while.   Indeed, our fleet was thought to
be in great danger, but we found all well.

21*st*.   The weather foul all this day also.
After dinner, about writing one thing or other
all day, and setting my papers in order, hearing, by letters that came hither in my absence,
that the Parliament had ordered all persons to
be secured, in order to a trial, that did sit as
judges in the late King's death, and all the
officers attending the Court.   Sir John Lenthall
moving in the House that all that had borne
arms against the King should be exempted from
pardon, he was called to the bar of the House,
and after a severe reproof, he was degraded his
knighthood.   At Court I find that all things
grow high.   The old clergy talk as being sure
of their lands again, and laugh at the Presby-
tery; and it is believed that the sales of the
King's and Bishops' lands will never be con-

firmed by Parliament, there being nothing now in any man's power to hinder them and the King from doing what they had a mind, but everybody willing to submit to anything. We expect every day to have the King and Duke on board as soon as it is fair. My Lord does nothing now, but offers all things to the pleasure of the Duke, as Lord High Admiral; so that I am at a loss what to do.

22*d.* Up, and trimmed by a barber that has not trimmed me yet, my Spaniard being on shore. News brought that the two Dukes are coming on board, which, by and by, they did, in a Dutch boat, the Duke of York in yellow trimmings, the Duke of Gloucester in grey and red. My Lord went in a boat to meet them; the Captain, myself, and others, standing at the entering port. So soon as they were entered, we shot the guns off round the fleet. After that, they went to view the ship all over, and were most exceedingly pleased with it. They seem to be very fine gentlemen. After that done, upon the quarter deck table, under the awning, the Duke of York, and my Lord, Mr. Coventry,[1] and I, spent an hour at allotting to

[1] Sir William Coventry, M. P., to whom Pepys became so warmly attached afterwards.

every ship their service, in their return to England; which being done they went to dinner, where the table was very full, the two Dukes at the upper end, my Lord Opdam next on one side, and my Lord on the other. Two guns given to every man while he was drinking the King's health, and so likewise to the Duke's health. I took down Monsieur d'Esquier to the great cabin below, and dined with him in state along with only one or two friends of his. All dinner, the harper belonging to Captain Sparling played to the Dukes. After dinner, the Dukes and my Lord to sea, the Vice and Rear-Admirals and I in a boat after them. After that done, they made to the shore in the Dutch boat that brought them, and I got into the boat with them; but the shore was full of people to expect their coming. When we came near the shore, my Lord left them, and come into his own boat, and General Pen and I with him; my Lord being very well pleased with this day's work. By the time we came on board again, news is sent us that the King is on shore; so my Lord fired all his guns round twice, and all the fleet after him, which, in the end, fell into disorder, which seemed very handsome. The gun over against my cabin I fired myself to the

King, which was the first time that he had been
saluted by **his own** ships since this change ; but,
holding my head too much over the gun, I had
almost spoiled my right eye. Nothing in the
world but giving of guns almost all this day.
In the evening we began to remove cabins ; I
to the carpenter's cabin, and Dr. Clerke with
me, who came on board this afternoon, having
been twice **ducked in the** sea to-day, and Mr.
North and John Pickering the like. Many of
the King's servants **came on** board to-night ;
and so many Dutch of all sorts come to see the
ship till **it** was quite dark, that we could **not**
pass by **one** another, which **was** a great trouble
to us all. **This** afternoon, Mr. Downing (who
was knighted yesterday by the King) was **here**
on board, and had **a ship** for his passage into
England with his lady and servants."

Good Mr. Pepys is so much occupied **with**
various duties that **he** had no opportunity of
visiting his family until the fourth week of the
following month, when we have this entry:
"*June* 22. **To bed** the first time since my
coming from **sea in** my own house, **for which**
God be praised." On the 8th of July, we have
this record : " To Whitehall Chapel, where **I**
got **in** with ease, by going before the **Lord**

Chancellor with Mr. Kipps. Here I heard very good musique, the first time I ever remember to have heard organs, and singing men in surplices, in my life. The Bishop of Chichester (King) preached before the King, and made a great flattering sermon, which I did not like, that the clergy should meddle with matters of state." The 10th is an important day with Samuel. It was the day that his patron and kinsman obtained the title of Earl of Sandwich, and was also important on other accounts. " This day I put on my new silk suit, the first that ever I wore in my life." It had further interest. Pepys had an eye for pretty women, and that day he took his wife to " a great wedding of Nan Hartlib's to Mynheer Roder, which was kept at Goring House with great state, cost, and able company. But among all the beauties there my wife was thought the greatest." — " Home, with my mind pretty quiet: not returning, as I said I would, to see the bride put to bed." A few months later, he says, " I did send for a cup of tee (a China drink) of which I never had drank before ; " [1]

---

[1] Tea was first introduced into Europe by the Dutch. probably about the beginning of the seventeenth century; but it was so little known in England, in the middle of that century,

and on the 22d of October, " Mr. Moore tells
me, among other things, that the Duke of York
is now sorry for his amour with my Lord
Chancellor's daughter,[1] who is now brought to
bed of a boy." On the 3d of January, 1661,
we find this entry : " To the Theatre, where
was acted ' Beggars Bush,' it being very well
done : and here the first time that ever I saw
women come upon the stage." On the 10th of
the same month, Samuel says, " By coach to
the Theatre and there saw ' The Scornful
Lady,' [2] now done by a woman, which makes
the play appear much better than ever it did to
me ; " and a few days afterwards, " To the
play-house, and there saw ' The Changeling,' [3]
the first time it hath been acted these twenty
years, and it takes exceedingly." From the
frequent entries of this character, it is very
evident that our diarist was a constant *habitué*
of the White-fryars and other London theatres.
February 23, Pepys writes, " This is now 28

that, in 1664, the East India Company presented two pounds
two ounces of it to the king as a rare, and therefore valuable
offering.

[1] Mary Hyde, afterwards Duchess of York.

[2] A comedy, by the literary partners and contemporaries of
Shakspeare — Beaumont and Fletcher.

[3] A tragedy, by Thomas Middleton.

years since I am born.   And blessed be God in
a full content, and a great hope to be a happy
man in all respects both to myself and friends.

27*th*. I called for a dish of fish, which we
had for dinner, this being the first day of Lent :
and I do intend to try whether I can keep it or
no."   As will be seen by the following confession, the honest old truepenny broke down : —

"28*th*. Notwithstanding my resolution, yet
for want of other victuals, I did eat flesh this
Lent, but am resolved to eat as little as I can."

For a philosopher and sinner, Samuel was
one of the most jovial dogs who ever lived, as
Sir Godfrey Kneller's portrait, from which our
frontispiece is engraved, fully indicates.   He
was very fond of *noctes ambrosianæ*, and could
have drank sack with Sir John of glorious
memory.   He sang and "made merry" with
his wife and friends in the public houses (as
was the custom of the day) to a prodigious
extent.   "Good drink," venison pastries, and
hot capons figure conspicuously in the pages of
our annalist.   Good Mistress Elizabeth was
not as companionable in his revelries as she
should have been, according to Samuel's rather
enlarged notions of sociality, and was doubtless
often an unwilling witness of his junketings

with female friends. Not a little of her discontent, which peeps forth in occasional bickerings, was the consequence of Pepys's fondness for these bacchanal pastimes, joined to that old and inveterate source of female misery — *spretœ injuria formœ;* for the lady was assuredly jealous, and not without reason ; whereat says Samuel, " I greatly troubled, but did presently satisfy her ! " The Secretary was much given to flirting with " mighty pretty women ; " with good Mistress Knipp ; with Mrs. Pierce, the surgeon's wife ; would squeeze the hand of a " pretty maid " whom he did not know, but whose beauty attracted him on his way to church, and frequently saluted with a kiss Rebecca Allen, the storekeeper's daughter at Chatham. Some of his meetings with this lady are very amusing. She appears first on the occasion of an official visit paid by him to Chatham in company with Sir William Batten, commissioner of the navy, who entertained, amongst others, " Mr. Allen and two daughters of his, both very tall, and the youngest very handsome, so much so I could not forbear to love her exceedingly." On the following day, he met her at an evening party, and accompanied the fair damsel to her father's house, she

seeming "to be desirous of his favors." He
staid there till "two o'clock in the morning,
and was most exceedingly merry, and had the
opportunity of *kissing* Mistress Rebecca very
often." Pretty well for a married man on a
second day's acquaintance! Again she appears
as Becky Allen, and finally as Mrs. Jewkes,
"who is a very fine, proper lady, as most I
know, and well dressed. . . . She and I to talk,
and then had our old stories up, and there I
had the liberty to salute her often, and she
mighty free in kindness to me." Few names
occur more frequently in the Diary than that of
Mrs. Knipp. She was an actress, the contemporary of Nell Gwynn, and Pepys's most intimate female friend. She was obviously the cause
of much disquietude to the Secretary's wife.
"After the play, we went into the house and
spoke with Knipp, who went abroad with us to
the Neat Houses in the way to Chelsy: and
there, in a box in a tree, we sat and sang, and
talked and eat: my wife out of humor, as she
always is, when this woman is by."

Samuel was indeed a sad dog, much given
to flirting with "mighty pretty women," and
evidently not less fond of osculatory salutations
than the stout old Roman who said to Lesbia,

" Give me a thousand kisses, then a hundred,
then another thousand, then a second hundred,
then a full thousand more, then a hundred.
Then, after we have interchanged many thousand, we will rub out the score, so that we
can't tell ourselves how many."

" *September* 7. Having appointed the young
ladies at the Wardrobe to go with them to the
play to-day, my wife and I took them to the
theatre, where we seated ourselves close to the
King, and Duke of York, and Madame Palmer,
which was great content; and indeed I can
never enough admire her beauty. And here
was ' Bartholomew Fayre,'[1] with the puppet-
show, acted to-day, which had not been these
forty years, (it being so satirical against puri-
tanism, they durst not till now, which is strange
they should already dare to do it, and the King
do countenance it,) but I do never a whit like
it the better for the puppets, but rather the worse.
Thence home with the ladies, it being by reason
of our staying a great while for the King's
coming, and the length of the play, near nine
o'clock before it was done.

11*th*. To Dr. Williams, who did carry me

---

[1] A comedy by Ben Jonson, first acted in 1614.

into his garden, where he hath abundance of
grapes: and he did show me how a dog that he
hath do kill all the cats that come thither to
kill his pigeons, and do afterwards bury them;
and do it with so much care that they shall be
quite covered; that if the tip of the tail hangs
out he will take up the cat again, and dig the
hole deeper. Which is very strange; and he
tells me, that he do believe that he hath killed
above 100 cats.

12*th.* To my Lady's to dinner at the Wardrobe; and in my way upon the Thames, I saw
the King's new pleasure-boat that is come now
for the King to take pleasure in above bridge;
and also two Gundaloes [1] that are lately brought,
which are very rich and fine.

24*th.* Letters from sea, that speak of my
Lord's being well; and his action, though not
considerable of any side, at Argier.

25*th.* Sir W. Pen told me that I need not
fear any reflection upon my Lord for their ill
success at Argier, for more could not be done.
To my Lord Crewe's, and dined with him,
where I was used with all imaginable kindness

---

[1] Gondolas. Davenant uses the expression, " Step into one
of your peascod boats, whose tilts are not so sumptuous as
the roofs of Gundaloes."

both from him and her. And I see that he is
afraid my **Lord's** reputation will a little suffer
in **common talk** by this late success; but there
is no help for it now. The Queen of England,
(as she is now owned **and** called) I hear doth
keep open Court, and distinct at Lisbone.

27*th.* At noon, met my wife at the Wardrobe; and there **dined,** where we found Captain
Country, (my little Captain that I loved, who
carried me to the **Sound,**) with some grapes
and melons from my Lord at Lisbone. **The**
first that ever **I** saw; but the grapes are rare
things. . . . Here we staid and supped too,
and after my wife had put up some of the
grapes in **a basket for** to be sent to the **King,**
we took **coach and home, where we found a**
hampire **of melons sent** to me also."

Occasionally, **if Pepys** witnesses **a play ill**
acted, he finds compensation in sitting near
some "pretty and ingenious lady," or is con-
soled by a gracious **nod** of recognition from the
Duchess of Cleveland (a woman, to use the
language of Hume, "prodigal, rapacious, dissolute, violent, revengeful"), or her beautiful
rival, *la belle* Stewart, afterwards Duchess of
Portsmouth, or from the **fair and** frail Nelly
Gwynn. **Early in January, 1663, Pepys re-**

cords that the Duke of York and his wife did
honor a play of Kelligrew's by their presence,
and did much edify the spectators by their con-
duct. " They did show," writes the immortal
journalist, " some impertinent and methought
unnatural dalliances there before the whole
world, such as kissing of hands, and leaning
one upon the other." The following entries
occur during the year 1664 : —

"*January 6th.* This morning I began a prac-
tice which I find by the ease I do it with, that I
shall continue, it saving me money and time :
that is, to trim myself with a razor : which
pleases me mightily.

30*th.* This evening I tore some old papers :
among others a romance which under the title
of ' Love a Cheate,' I began ten years ago at
Cambridge : and reading it over to-night, I
liked it very well, and wondered a little at myself at my vein at that time when I wrote it,
doubting that I cannot do so well now if I
would try.

March 18*th.* Up betimes, and walked to my
brother's, where a great while putting things in
order against anon ; and so to Wotton, my shoe-
maker, and there got a pair of shoes blacked on
the soles against anon for me ; so to my broth-

er's. To church,[1] and, with the grave-maker, chose a place for my brother to lie in, just under my mother's pew. But to see how a man's tombes (bones?) are at the mercy of such a fellow, that for sixpence he would, as his own words were, ' I will justle them together but I will make room for him; ' speaking of the fulness of the middle aisle, where he was to lie ; and that he would, for my father's sake, do my brother, that is dead, all the civility he can ; which was to disturb other corps that are not quite rotten, to make room for him ; and methought his manner of speaking it was very remarkable ; as of a thing that now was in his power to do a man a courtesy or not. I dressed myself, and so did my servant Besse ; and so to my brother's again ; whither, though invited, as the custom is, at one or two o'clock, they come not till four or five. . But, at last, one after another, they come, many more than I bid : and my reckoning that I bid was one hundred and twenty ; but I believe there was nearer one hundred and fifty. Their service was six biscuits apiece, and what they pleased of burnt

[1] St. Bride's, of which Richard Pearson, D. D., the vicar, officiated at the funeral. " March 18, 1663-4, Mr. Thomas Pepys." — *Burial Register of St. Bride's, Fleet Street.*

claret.   My cousin Joyce Norton kept the wine
and cakes above ; and did give out to them that
served, who had white gloves given them.   But,
above all, I am beholden to Mrs. Holden, who
was most kind, and did take mighty pains not
only in getting the house and everything else
ready, but this day in going up and down to see
the house filled and served, in order to mine and
their great content, I think : the men sitting by
themselves in some rooms, and the women by
themselves in others, very close, but yet room
enough.   Anon to church, walking out into the
street to the conduit, and so across the street :
and had a very good company along with the
corpse.   And, being come to the grave as above,
Dr. Pierson, the minister of the parish, did read
the service for burial ; and so I saw my poor
brother laid into the grave : and so all broke
up, and I and my wife, and Madam Turner and
her family, to her brother's, and by and by fell
to a barrel of oysters, cake, and cheese, of
Mr. Honiwood's, with him, in his chamber and
below, being too merry for so late a sad work.
But, Lord ! to see how the world makes nothing
of the memory of a man, an hour after he is
dead !   And, indeed, I must blame myself ; for,
though at the sight of him dead and dying, I

had real grief for a while, while he was in my
sight, yet presently after, and ever since, I have
had very little grief indeed for him.

19*th*. My wife and I alone, having a good
hen, with eggs, to dinner, with great content.
Then to my brother's, where I spent the afternoon in paying some of the charges of the
burial.

21*st*. This day the Houses of Parliament
met; and the King met them, with the Queen
with him. And he made a speech to them:
among other things, discoursing largely of the
plots abroad against him and the peace of the
kingdom; and that the dissatisfied party had
great hopes upon the effect of the Act for a Tri-
ennial Parliament granted by his father, which
he desired them to peruse, and, I think, repeal.
So the Houses did retire to their own House,
and did order the Act to be read to-morrow
before them; and I suppose it will be repealed,
though I believe much against the will of a good
many that sit there.

23*d*. To the Trinity House, and there dined
very well: and good discourse among the old
men. Among other things, they observed, that
there are but two seamen in the Parliament,
viz., Sir W. Batten and Sir W. Pen, and not

above twenty or thirty merchants; which is a strange thing in an island. In the evening, my Lady Jemimah, Paulina, and Madame Pickering came to see us, but my wife would not be seen, being unready. Very merry with them; they mightily talking of their thrifty living for a fortnight before their mother came to town, and other such simple talk, and of their merry life at Brampton, at my father's this winter.

April 26th. My wife gone this afternoon to the burial of my she-cousin Scott, a good woman: and it is a sad consideration how the Pepys decay, and nobody almost that I know in a present way of increasing them."

On the last day of May, our worthy and observant annalist mentions "that upon Sunday night, being the King's birthday, the King was at my Lady Castlemaine's lodgings, over the shelter-gate at Lambert's lodgings, dancing with fiddlers all night most."

Pepys also remarks that he went with his friend Mr. Povy, who, Evelyn, in his Diary, July 1, 1664, informs us, lived in Lincoln's Inn, home to dinner, "where extraordinary cheer; and after dinner, up and down to see his house. And in a word, methinks, for his perspective in the little closet: his room floored above with woods of several colors, like, but above the best cabinet-work I ever saw : his grotto and vault, with his bottles of wine, and a well therein, to keep them cool : his furniture of all sorts : his bath at the top of the house, good pictures, and his manner of eating and drinking, do surpass all that ever I did see of one man in all my life."

Should any dyspeptic, who is unable to indulge in good cheer, and therefore feels a contempt for meat and wine, or any disciple of Father Mathew, be inclined to take exception to Samuel's constant recurrence to the subject of eating and drinking, we would say, that he is in this respect kept in countenance by the customs of the age in which he lived. Lady Fanshawe, a contemporary, in her delightful Memoirs, constantly refers, with almost as much gusto and genuine relish, to the gratification of feasting, as does the worthy Pepys. This woman of wit and beauty, who, in a corrupt and dissolute age was a true and virtuous wife, displays the same love of pomp and ceremony, the same fondness for dress and show, which possessed the lively Secretary. As to her honest likings for the good things of this life, — which are confessed with the most engaging *naïveté*, — she never stops at

7

a town, or describes a country, without a particular and minute inventory of its delicious products and artificial luxuries. Lord Clarendon, another of Pepys's contemporaries, confessed that he "indulged his palate very much, and even took some delight in eating and drinking, but without any approach to luxury;" while all will remember the incident of Milton praising his wife for the well-cooked dish. To come down a few score years, who does not remember Dr. Johnson's partialities in eating and drinking, Scott's love for the dishes of his native land, or dear Charles Lamb's exquisite relish of roast pig?

Samuel certainly was no saint, and seems to have been a perfect giant in tavernizing and junketing generally, if we may judge by the almost daily and certainly weekly episodes in which fat capons, venison pasties, or mulled sack, and other "good drink," alternate with allusions to kissing Mistress Knipp, or "a pretty maid;" but, as Horace has it, "Aliquando bonus dormitat," &c. We cannot claim for him much resemblance to the heroes of novels, or the subjects of biography, who are too generally described as

"Faultless monsters, whom the world ne'er saw."

Indeed, Kneller's portrait, with the high bluff cheeks and double chin, proclaims Pepys to have been anything but an anchorite, but rather a man who would have sympathized with the Illinois farmer, who told Richard Cobden, while entertaining the eminent Englishman with some fine peach brandy, that he had laid away two hundred barrels of it for his old age! "Certainly," as the great advocate of free trade afterwards remarked to the writer, "a most extraordinary provision for his declining years."

Something too much of this. Let us now continue our citations from the Diary:—

"*June* 1*st*. By water to Woolwich, all the way reading Mr. Spencer's[1] book of Prodigies, which is most ingeniously writ, both for matter and style. Southwell,[2] Sir W. Pen's friend, tells me the very sad news of my Lord Teviott's and nineteen more commission officers being killed at Tangier by the Moores,[3] by an ambush

[1] John Spencer, D. D., who died in 1695, was also the author of a celebrated work, *De Legibus Hebræorum.* His *Discourse concerning Prodigies* first appeared in 1663; the 2d edition, of 1665, contains likewise a *Discourse concerning Vulgar Prophecies.*

[2] Afterwards Sir Robert Southwell.

[3] The particulars of the loss at **Tangiers** is given in *The Intelligencer*, 6th June, 1664.

of the enemy upon them, while they were sur-
veying their lines: which is very sad, and he
says afflicts the King much. To the King's
house, and saw 'The Silent Woman;' but
methought not so well done or so good a play
as I formerly thought it to be. Before the play
was done, it fell such a storm of hail, that we,
in the middle of the pit, were fain to rise; and
all the house in a disorder.[1]

2*d*. To a Committee of Tangier about providing provisions, money, and men; but it is
strange to see how poorly and brokenly things
are done of the greatest consequence, and how
soon the memory of this great man is gone, or,
at least, out of mind by the thoughts of who
goes next, which is not yet known. My Lord
of Oxford, Muskerry, and several others, are
discoursed of. It seems my Lord Teviott's
design was to go a mile and a half out of the
town, to cut down a wood in which the enemy
did use to lie in ambush. He had sent several
spies; but all brought word that the way was
clear, and so might be for anybody's discovery

---

1 The Blackfriar's Theatre was entirely roofed over, and
had a pit, instead of a mere enclosed yard; whilst the stage
portion alone of the public playhouses was protected from the
weather. The house was lighted by a cupola.

of an enemy before you are upon them. There
they were all snapped, he and all his officers,
and about two hundred men, as they say ; there
being left now in the garrison but four captains.
This happened the 3d of May last, being not
before that day twelvemonth of his entering
into his government there ; but, at his going
out in the morning, he said to some of his officers, ' Gentlemen, let us look to ourselves, for
it was this day three years that so many brave
Englishmen were knocked on the head by the
Moores, when Fines[1] made his sally out.'

3d. At the Committee for Tangier all the
afternoon — the Duke of York and Mr. Coventry, for ought I see, being the only two that do
anything like men ; Prince Rupert do nothing
but swear and laugh, with an oath or two.

4th. I went forth with J. Noble, who tells
me that he will secure us against Cave — that
though he knows, and can prove it, yet nobody
else can prove it, to be Tom's child ; that the
bond was made by one Hudson, a scrivener,
next to the Fountain tavern, in the Old Bayly ;
that the children were born, and christened, and
entered in the parish-book of St. Sepulchre's,

---

[1] Major Fiennes, whose regiment formed part of the garrison at Tangier.

by the name of Anne and Elizabeth Taylor; and he will give us security against Cave if we pay him the money. To the Duke, and was giving him an account how matters go, and of the necessity there is of a power to press sea-men, without which we cannot really raise men for this fleet of twelve sail, besides that it will assert the King's power of pressing, which at present is somewhat doubted, and will make the Dutch believe that we are in earnest. To the Committee of Tangier all the afternoon, where still the same confused doings, and my Lord Fitz-Harding now added to the Committee, which will signify much. Mr. Coventry discoursing this noon about Sir W. Batten, what a sad fel-low he is, told me how the King told him the other day how Sir W. Batten, being in the ship with him and Prince Rupert when they expected to fight with Warwicke, did walk up and down sweating, with a napkin under his throat to dry up his sweat; and that Prince Rupert, being a most jealous man, and particularly of Batten, do walk up and down swearing bloodily to the King, that Batten had a mind to betray them to-day, and that the napkin was a signal: 'But, by God,' says he, ' if things go ill, the first thing I will do is to shoot him.' He discoursed largely and bravely to me concerning the different sort of valors, the active and passive valor. For the latter, he brought as an instance General Blake, who, in the defending of Taunton and Lyme for the Parliament, did, through his sober sort of valor, defend it the most *opiniastrément* that ever any man did anything; and yet never was the man that ever made an attaque by land or sea, but rather avoided it on all, even fair occasions. On the other side, Prince Rupert, the boldest attaquer in the world for personal courage: and yet, in the defending of Bristol, no man ever did anything worse, he wanting the patience and seasoned head to consult and advise for defence, and to bear with the evils of a siege. The like he says of my Lord Teviott, who was the boldest adventurer of his person in the world; and from a mean man in few years was come to this greatness of command and repute only by the death of all his officers, he many times having the luck of being the only survivor of them all, by venturing upon services for the King of France that nobody else would; and yet no man upon a defence, he being all fury and of no judgment in a fight. He tells me, above all, of the Duke of York, that he is more himself and more of judgment is at hand in him,

in the middle of a desperate service, than at
other times, as appeared in the business of Dun-
kirke, wherein no man ever did braver things,
or was in hotter service in the close of that day,
being surrounded with enemies ; and then, contrary to the advice of all about him, his counsel
carried himself and the rest through them safe,
by advising that he might make his passage
with but a dozen with him : " For," says he,
" the enemy cannot move after me so fast with
a great body, and with a small one we shall
be enough to deal with them ; " and, though he
is a man naturally martial to the hottest degree,
yet a man that never in his life talks one word
of himself or service of his own, but only that
he saw such or such a thing, and lays it down
for a maxim that a Hector can have no courage.   He told me also, as a great instance of
some men, that the Prince of Condé's excellence
is, that there not being a more furious man in
the world, danger in fight never disturbs him
more than just to make him civil, and to command in words of great obligation to his officers
and men, but without any the least disturbance
in his judgment or spirit.

   6th.   By barge with Sir W. Batten to Trinity
House.   Here were my Lord Sandwich, Mr.

Coventry, my Lord Craven, and others. A great dinner, and good company. Mr. **Prin**, also, who would not drink any health, no, not the King's, **but** sat down with his hat on all the while; but nobody took **notice of it** to him at all.

8th. With Creed talking **of many things,** among others of my Lord's going so often to Chelsey, and **he do tell me** that his daughters do **perceive all, and do hate the** place and the young woman, Mrs. **Betty Becke**; for my Lord who sent them **thither, only for a disguise for his** going thither, **will come** under a pretence to see them, **and pack them out of doors to** the Parke, **and stay behind with her: but now** the **young ladies are gone to their mother to** Kensington.

11th. With **my wife only to take the air, it** being very warm **and pleasant, to Bowe and** Old Ford: **and thence to Hackney. There** light, and played at shuffleboard, eat cream and good cherries; **and so with good refreshment** home.

13th. Spent the **whole morning reading of some** old Navy books; wherein the order that was **observed in the Navy then, above what it is now,** is very observable. Mr. **Coventry did talk of**

a History of the Navy of England, how fit it
were to be writ; and he did say that it hath
been in his mind to propose to me the writing
of the History of the late Dutch war, which I
am glad to hear, it being a thing I much desire,
and sorts mightily with my genius ; and if done
well, may recommend me much.   So he says
he will get me an order for making of searches
to all records, &c., in order thereto, and I shall
take great delight in doing of it.

14th. By coach to Kensington.   In the way
overtaking Mr. Laxton, the apothecary, with his
wife and daughters — very fine young lasses —
in a coach ; and so both of us to my Lady Sandwich, who hath lain this fortnight here, at
Dean Hodge's.[1]   Much company come hither
to-day — my Lady Carteret, &c., Sir William
Wheeler and his lady, and, above all, Mr. Becke,
of Chelsey, and wife and daughter, my Lord's
mistress, and one that hath not one good feature
in her face, and yet is a fine lady, of a fine taille,
and very well carriaged, and mighty discreet.
I took all the occasion I could to discourse with

---

1 Thomas Hodges, vicar of Kensington, and rector of St.
Peter's, Cornhill. He had been, in September, 1661, preferred
to the deanery of Hereford, which he held with his two livings
till his death, in 1672.

the young ladies in her company to give occasion to her to talk, which now and then she did, and that mighty finely, and is, I perceive, a woman of such an air, as I wonder the less at my Lord's favor to her, and I dare warrant him she hath brains enough to entangle him. Two or three hours we were in her company, going into Sir H. Finche's garden,[1] and seeing the fountain, and singing there with the ladies; and a mighty fine cool place it is, with a great laver of water in the middle, and the bravest place for music I ever heard. After much mirth, discoursing to the ladies in defence of the city against the country or court, and giving them occasion to invite themselves to-morrow to me to dinner to my venison pasty, I got their mother's leave, and so good night, very well pleased with my day's work, and, above all, that I have seen my Lord's mistress.

15th. I got Captain Witham to tell me the whole story of my Lord Teviott's misfortune; for he was upon the guard with his horse near the town, when at a distance he saw the enemy appear upon a hill, a mile and a half off, and made up to them, and with much ado escaped himself; but what became of my Lord he

---

1 Now Kensington Gardens.

neither knows nor thinks that anybody but the
enemy can tell. Our loss was about four hundred. But he tells me that the greater wonder
is, that my Lord Teviott met no sooner with
such a disaster; for every day he did commit
himself to more probable danger than this, for
now he had the assurance of all his scouts that
there was no enemy thereabouts; whereas, he
used every day to go out with two or three with
him, to make his discoveries in greater danger,
and yet the man that could not endure to have
anybody else to go a step out of order to endanger himself. He concludes him to be the man
of the hardest fate to lose so much honor at one
blow that ever was. His relation being done,
he parted; and I home. At home, to look
after things for dinner. And anon at noon
comes Mr. Creed by chance, and by and by the
three young ladies: and very merry we were
with our pasty, very well baked; and a good
dish of roasted chickens; pease, lobsters,
strawberries. And after dinner to cards: and
about five o'clock, by water down to Greenwich; and up to the top of the hill, and there
played upon the ground at cards. And so to
the Cherry Garden,[1] and then by water singing

---

[1] The Cherry Garden was at Rotherbithe.

finely to the Bridge, and there landed;[1] and so took boat again, and to Somerset House. And by this time, the tide being against us, it was past ten of the clock; and such a troublesome passage, in regard to my Lady Paulina's fearfulness, that in all my life I never did see any poor wretch in that condition. Being come hither, there waited for them their coach; but, it being so late, I doubted what to do how to get them home. After half an hour's stay in the street, I sent my wife home by coach with Mr. Creed's boy: and myself and Creed in the coach home with them. But, Lord! the fear that my Lady Paulina was in every step of the way: and indeed, at this time of the night, it was no safe thing to go that road; so that I was even afraid myself, though I appeared otherwise.[2] We come safe, however, to their house; where we knocked them up, my Lady and all the family being in bed. So put

---

[1] To avoid the danger of what was called "shooting the bridge."

[2] We have here a curious picture of the dreadful state of the streets in London in 1664. No improvement of what they were a century before, when they were described as "very foul, full of pits and sloughs, very perilous and noxious" (Knight's London), appears to have taken place. The alarm of Lady Paulina and Pepys at night was not surprising.

them into doors; and, leaving them with the
maids, bade them **good** night. Then into the
town [1] — Creed and I, it being about twelve
o'clock and past: and to several houses — inns,
but could get no lodging, all being in bed. At
last, we found some people drinking and roar-
ing; and, after drinking, got an ill bed.

16th. **I** lay in my drawers, and stockings,
and waistcoat till five of the clock, and so up;
and, being well pleased with our frolic, walked
to **Knightsbridge**, and there eat a mess of cream,
and so to St. James's, and I to Whitehall, and
took coach, and found my wife well got home
last night, and now in bed. The talk upon the
'Change is, that De Ruyter is dead, with fifty
men of his own ship, of the plague, at Cales:
that the Holland Embassador here do endeavor
to sweeten us with fair words: and things like
to be peaceable. With my cousin Richard
Pepys upon the 'Change, about supplying us
with bewpers [2] from **Norwich**, which I should
be glad of, if cheap.

[1] Kensington.

[2] This word is used by Spenser for companions or equals.
Pieces of cloth, each containing twenty-five yards, were
known by the name of *beaupers;* but the word has fallen into
disuse. It appears from one of the Pepys papers of a later
date that bewpers were used as a material for flags.

20*th*. I to the Duke, where we did our usual business. And among other discourse of the Dutch, he was merrily saying how they print that Prince Rupert, Duke of Albemarle, and my Lord Sandwich, are to be Generals: and soon after is to follow them 'Vieux Pen:' and so the Duke called him in mirth Old Pen.[1] They have, it seems, lately wrote to the King, to assure him that their setting-out ships was only to defend their fishing-trade, and to stay near home — not to annoy the King's subjects: and to desire that he would do the like with his ships: which the King laughs at, but yet is troubled they should think him such a child, to suffer them to bring home their fish and East India Company's ships, and then they will not care for us. Meeting Pickering, he tells us how my Lady last week went to see Mrs. Becke, the mother; and by and by the daughter come in, but that my Lady do say herself, as he says, that she knew not for what reason, for she never knew they had a daughter, which I do not believe. She was troubled, and her heart did rise as soon as she appeared, and seems the most ugly woman that ever she saw. This, if true, were strange, but I believe it is

---

[1] He was only forty-two years of age.

not. To my Lord's lodgings : and was merry with the young ladies, who make a great story of their appearing before their mother the morning after we carried them, the last week, home so late ; and that their mother took it very well, at least, without any anger. Here I heard how the rich widow, my Lady Gold, is married to one Neale,[1] after he had received a box on the ear by her brother,[2] who was there a sentinel, in behalf of some courtier, at the door ; but made him draw, and wounded him. She called Neale up to her, and sent for a priest, married presently, and went to bed. The brother sent to the Court, and had a sergeant sent for Neale ; but Neale sent for him up to be seen in bed, and she owned him for her husband : and so all is past. It seems Sir H. Bennet did look after her. My Lady very pleasant. After dinner come in Sir Thomas Crewe and Mr. Sidney (Montagu), lately come from France, who is grown a little, and a pretty youth he is, but not so improved as they did give him out to be, but like a child still. But yet I can perceive he hath good parts and good inclinations.

21*st*. Meeting Mr. Moore, I perceive by him

---

[1] Thomas Neale.   [2] **She had** four brothers.

my Lord's business of his family and estate
goes very ill, and runs in debt mightily. I
would to God I were clear of it, both as to my
own money and the bond of £1000, which I
stand debtor for him in, to my cousin Thomas
Pepys.

22d. To the 'Change and Coffee House,
where great talk of the Dutch preparing of
sixty sail of ships. The plague grows mightily
among them, both at sea and land.

23d. W. Howe was with me this afternoon,
to desire some things to be got ready for my
Lord against his going down to his ship, which
will be soon ; for it seems the King and both
the Queens intend to visit him. The Lord
knows how my Lord will get out of this
charge ; for Mr. Moore tells me to-day that he
is £10,000 in debt : and this will, with many
other things, that daily grow upon him, while
he minds his pleasure as he do, set him further
backward.

24th. To the City granaries, where, it seems,
every company have their granary,[1] and obliged

[1] From the commencement of the reign of Henry VIII., or
perhaps earlier, it was the custom of the city of London to
provide against scarcity by requiring each of the chartered
companies to keep in store a certain quantity of corn, which
was to be renewed from time to time, and when required for

to keep such a quantity of corn always there, or, at a time of scarcity, to issue it at so much a bushel; and a fine thing it is to see their stores of all sorts, for piles for the bridge, and for pipes. To White Hall; and Mr. Pierce showed me the Queen's bed-chamber, and her closet where she had nothing but some pretty pious pictures, and books of devotion; and her holy water at her head as she sleeps, with a clock by her bed-side, wherein a lamp burns that tells her the time of the night at any time. Thence with him to the Park, and there met the Queen coming from Chapel, with her Maids of Honor, all in silver-lace gowns again; which is new to me, and that which I did not think would have been brought up again. Thence he carried me to the King's closet: where such variety of pictures, and other things of value and rarity, that I was properly confounded, and enjoyed no pleasure in the sight of them; which is the only time in my life that ever I was so at a loss for pleasure, in the greatest plenty of objects to give it me.

that purpose, produced in the market for sale, at such times and prices, and in such quantities, as the Lord Mayor or Common Council should direct. (See the report of a case in the Court of Chancery, Attorney-General *v.* Haberdashers' Company, Mylne and Keen's Reports.)

26*th*. (Lord's Day.) At my Lord Sandwich's; where his little daughter, my Lady Katherine, was brought, who is lately come from my father's at Brampton, to have her cheeke looked after, which is and hath long been sore. But my Lord will rather have it be as it is, with a scar in her face, than endanger it being worse by tampering. I went home, and with Creed called at several churches, which, God knows, are supplied with very young men, and the churches very empty; and at our own church looked in, and there heard one preach whom Sir William Penn brought, which he desired us yesterday to hear, that had been his chaplain in Ireland: a very silly fellow. After dinner, a frolic took us, we would go this afternoon to the Hope; so my wife dressed herself, and, with good victuals and drink, we took boat presently, and the tide with us, got down, but it was night, and the tide spent by the time we got to Gravesend: so there we stopped, but went not on shore, only Creed, to get some cherries, and sent a letter to the Hope, where the Fleet lies. And so, it being rainy, and thundering mightily, and lightning, we returned with great pleasure home, about twelve o'clock — Creed telling pretty stories in the boat. He lay with me all night.

27*th*. To Paul's Churchyard, and there saw Sir Harry Spillman's book,[1] and I bespoke it and others.

28*th*. Put on a half shirt first this summer, it being very hot; and yet so ill-tempered I am grown, that I am afraid I shall catch cold, while all the world is afraid to melt away. To the Mitre, and there comes Dr. Burnett to us: and there I begun to have his advice about my disease, and then invited him to my house; and I am resolved to put myself into his hands.

29*th*. Mr. Shepley tells me how my brave dog I did give him, going out betimes one morning, to Huntingdon, was set upon by five other dogs, and worried to pieces, of which I am a little, and he the most sorry I ever saw man for such a thing. To Westminster, to see Dean Honiwood, whom I had not visited a great while. He is a good-natured, but a very weak man, yet a Dean, and a man in great esteem. My Lady[2] and I sat two hours, alone, talking of the condition of her family's being greatly in debt, and many children now coming up to provide for. I did give her my sense very plainly of it, which she took well, and carried further than myself,

---

[1] Glossarium Archaiologicum.
[2] Sandwich.

to the bemoaning their condition, and remembering how finely things were ordered about six years ago, when I lived there, and my Lord at sea every year.

30th. By water to Woolwich, and walked back from Woolwich to Greenwich all alone; saw a man that had a cudgel in his hand, and, though he told me he labored in the King's yard, and many other good arguments that he is an honest man, yet, God forgive me! I did doubt he might knock me on the head behind with his club. But I got safe home. Great doubts yet whether the Dutch war go on or no. The fleet ready in the Hope, of twelve sail. The King and Queens go on board, they say, on Saturday next. Young children of my Lord Sandwich gone with their maids from my mother's, which troubles me — it being, I hear, from Mr. Shepley, with great discontent, saying that, though they buy good meate, yet can never have it before it stinks, which I am ashamed of.

July 1*st.* Comes Dr. Burnett, who did write me down some direction what to do, but not with the satisfaction I expected. I did give him a piece, with good hopes, however, that his advice will be of use to me. Upon the 'Change, this day, I saw how uncertain the temper of the people is, that from our discharging about 200 that lay idle, having nothing to do, upon some of our ships, which were ordered to be fitted for service, and their works are now done, the town do talk that the King discharges all his men — 200 yesterday, and 800 to-day — and that now he hath got 100,000*l.* in his hand, he values not a Dutch war. But I undeceived a great many, telling them how it is.

3*d.* (Lord's Day.) At noon, to dinner, where the remains of yesterday's venison, and a couple of brave green geese, which we are fain to eat alone, because they will not keep, which troubled us. Thundering and lightning all the evening, and this year have had the most thunder and lightning, they say, of any in man's memory, and so it is, it seems, in France and everywhere.

4*th.* This day the King and the Queen went to visit my Lord Sandwich and the fleet, going forth in the Hope.[1]

6*th.* Up very betimes, and my wife also, and

---

[1] Their Majesties were treated at Tilbury Hope by the Earl of Sandwich, returning the same day, abundantly satisfied, both with the dutiful respects of that honorable person, and with the excellent condition of all matters committed to his charge. — *The Newes,* 7th July, 1664.

got us ready; and about eight o'clock, having got some bottles of wine and beer, and neat's tongues, we went to our barge at the Tower, where Mr. Pierce and his wife, and a kinswoman and his sister, and Mrs. Clerke and her sister, and cousin, were to expect us; and so set out for the Hope, all the way down playing at cards, and other sports, spending our time pretty merry. Come to the Hope about one, and there showed them all the ships, and had a collation of anchovies, gammon, &c., and after an hour's stay or more, embarked again for home; and so to cards, and other sports, till we come to Greenwich, and there Mrs. Clerke, and my wife and I, on shore, to an alehouse, and so to the barge again, having shown them the King's pleasure-boat: and so home to the Bridge, bringing night home with us: so to the Tower wharf, and home, being very well pleased to-day with the company, especially Mrs. Pierce, who continues her complexion as well as ever, and hath at this day, I think, the best complexion that ever I saw on any woman, young or old, or child either, all days of my life. Also, Mrs. Clerke's kinswoman sings very prettily, but is very confident in it — Mrs. Clerke herself witty, but spoils all in being so conceited, and

making so great a flutter with a few fine clothes,
and some bad tawdry things worn with them.
The reason of Dr. Clerke's not being here was,
the King being sick last night, and let blood,
and so he durst not come away to-day.

7*th.*   To White Hall, and there found the
Duke and twenty more reading their commission (of which I am, and was also sent to,
to come) for the Royal Fishery, which is very
large, and a very serious charter it is; but the
Company generally so ill fitted for so serious a
work, that I do much fear it will come to little.
Home, calling for my new books, viz., Sir H.
Spillman's 'Whole Glossary,' Scapula's 'Lexi-
con,' and Shakespeare's plays, which I have got
money out of my stationer's bills to pay for.
The King is pretty well, to-day.

8*th.*   To the binder's, and directed the doing
of my Chaucer, though they were not full neat
enough for me, but pretty well it is; and thence
to the clasp-maker's to have it clasped and
bossed.

9*th.*   To a Committee for Fishing; but the
first thing was swearing to be true to the Company; and we were all sworn, but a great dispute we had, which, methought, is very ominous
to the Company — some, that we should swear

to be true to the best of our power; and others, to the best of our understanding — and carried in the last, though in that we are the least able to serve the Company, because we would not be obliged to attend the business when we can, but when we list.

10*th.* (Lord's Day.) Up, and by water, towards noon, to Somersett House, and walked to my Lord Sandwich's, and there dined with my lady and the children. After dinner, took our leaves, and my wife hers, in order to her going to the country to-morrow. My Lady showed us my Lady Castlemaine's [1] picture, finely done, given my Lord; and a most beautiful picture it is. Thence with my Lady Jemimah, and Mr. Sidney [Montagu], to St. Gyles's church, and there heard a long, poor sermon. Thence set them down, and in their coach to Kate Joyce's christening, where much company and good service of sweetmeats; and, after an hour's stay, left them, and in my Lord's coach — his noble, rich coach — home.

11*th.* Betimes up this morning, and, getting ready, we by coach to Holborne, where, at nine o'clock, they set out, and I and my man Will on

---

[1] This fine portrait is still at Hinchingbrooke, and in very good preservation.

horseback by my wife to Barnett; a very pleasant day; and there dined with her company,
which was very good — a pretty gentlewoman
with her, that goes but to Huntingdon, and a
neighbor to us in town.   Here we staid two
hours, and then parted for all together, and my
poor wife I shall soon want, I am sure.   Thence
I and Will to see the Wells,[1] half a mile off, and
there I drunk three glasses, and walked, and
come back and drunk two more : and so we
rode home, round by Kingsland, Hackney, and
Mile End, till we were quite weary; and, not
being very well, I betimes to bed.   About eleven
o'clock, knowing what money I have in the
house, and hearing a noise, I begun to sweat
worse and worse, till I melted almost to water.
I rung, and could not in half an hour make
either of the wenches hear me; and this made
me fear the more, lest they might be gagged;
and then I begun to think that there was some
design in a stone being flung at the window over
our stairs this evening, by which the thiefes
meant to try what looking there would be after
them, and know our company.   These thoughts
and fears I had, and do hence apprehend the
fears of all rich men that are covetous, and have

1 The mineral spring at East Barnett.

much money by them. At last, Jane rose, and then I understand it was only the dog wants a lodging, and so made a noise.

12*th.* Called up by my Lord Peterborough's gentleman, about getting his **Lord's** money to-day of Mr. Povy, wherein I took **such** order, that it was paid, and I had my 50*l.* brought me, which comforts my heart. Dined alone; sad for want of company, and not being very well, and know not how to eat alone.

Aug. 26*th.* Mr. Pen,[1] Sir William's son, is come back from France, and come to visit my wife. A most modish person grown, she says a fine gentleman.

Sept. 21*st.* **Home to bed:** having got a strange cold in my head, by flinging off my hat[2] at dinner, and sitting with the wind at **my back.**

Nov. 21*st.* This day for certain **news is** come that Teddeman hath brought in eighteen or twenty Dutchmen, merchants, their Bour-deaux fleet, and two men-of-war to Portsmouth. And I had letters this afternoon, that three are brought into the **Downes** and Dover, so that **the** war is begun: God give a good end to it.

---

[1] William Penn, the founder of Pennsylvania.

[2] In Lord Clarendon's Essay on the decay of respect paid to age, he says, that in his younger days he never kept his hat on before those older than himself, except at dinner.

Dec. 21*st*.　To Mrs. Turner, to Salisbury
Court, and with her a little; and carried her,
the porter staying for me, our eagle, which she
desired the other day, and we were glad to be
rid of her.　They are much pleased with her.
My Lord Sandwich this day writes me word
that he hath seen, at Portsmouth, the Comet,
and says it is the most extraordinary thing he
ever saw.

22*d*.　Met with a copy of verses, mightily
commended by some gentlemen there, of my
Lord Mordaunt's, in excuse of his going to sea
this late expedition, with the Duke of York.
But, Lord! they are sorry things; only a Lord
made them.　Thence, to the 'Change; and
there, among the merchants, I hear fully the
news of our being beaten to dirt at Guinny, by
De Ruyter, with his fleet.　The particulars, as
much as by Sir G. Carteret afterwards I heard,
I have said in a letter to my Lord Sandwich
this day at Portsmouth; it being most wholly
to the utter ruin of our Royal Company, and
reproach and shame to the whole nation, as
well as justification to them, in their doing
wrong to no man as to his private property,
only taking whatever is found to belong to the
Company, and nothing else.　Dined at the Dol-

phin — Sir G. Carteret, Sir J. Minnes, Sir W. Batten, and I, with Sir William Boreman, and Sir Theophilus Biddulph [1] and others, Commissioners of the Sewers, about our place below to lay masts in. But coming a little too soon, I out again, and took boat down to Redriffe ; and just in time within two minutes, and saw the new vessel of Sir William Petty's launched, the King and Duke being there. It swims and looks finely, and I believe will do well. Coming away back immediately to dinner, where a great deal of good discourse, and Sir G. Carteret's discourse of this Guinny business, with great displeasure at the loss of our honor there, and do now confess that the trade brought all these troubles upon us between the Dutch and us.

24*th*. Having sat up all night till past two o'clock this morning, our porter, being appointed, comes and tells us that the bellman tells him that the Star is seen upon Tower Hill; so I, that had been all night setting in order all my old papers in my chamber, did leave off all, and my boy and I to Tower Hill, it being a most fine, bright, moonshine night, and a great frost,

---

[1] Sir Theophilus Biddulph, of Westcombe, Kent, who had been previously knighted, was made a Baronet, 2d November, 1664. He was then serving in Parliament for Lichfield.

but no Comet to be seen. At noon to the 'Change, to the Coffee-house ; and there heard Sir Richard Ford tell the whole story of our defeat at Guinny, wherein our men are guilty of the most horrid cowardice and perfidiousness, as he says and tells it, that ever Englishmen were. Captain Raynolds, that was the only commander of any of the King's ships there, was shot at by De Ruyter, with a bloody flag flying. He, instead of opposing, which, indeed, had been to no purpose, but only to maintain honor, did poorly go on board himself, to ask what De Ruyter would have, and so yield whatever Ruyter would desire. The King and Duke are highly vexed at it, it seems, and the business deserves it. I saw the Comet,[1] which now, whether worn away or no, I know not, appears not with a tail, but only is larger and duller than any other star, and is come to rise betimes, and to make a great arch, and is gone quite to a new place in the heavens than it was before ; but I hope, in a clearer night, something more will be seen.

25*th.* (Lord's Day.) To Mr. Rawlinson's

[1] It is one of the twenty-four comets of which the observations have been collected in Halley's *Astronomiæ Cometicæ Synopsis.*

church,[1] where I heard a good sermon of one that I remember was at Paul's with me — his name Maggett; and very great store of fine women there is in this church, more than I know anywhere else about us.

26*th.* To Sir W. Batten's, where Mr. Coventry and all our families here, and Sir R. Ford and his, and a great feast, and good discourse and merry, and so home to bed, where my wife and people innocently at cards, very merry. I to bed, leaving them to their sport, and blindman's buff.

27*th.* 'Up at seven, and to Deptford and Woolwich in a galley; the Duke calling me out of a barge in which the King was with him, to know whither I was going. I told him to Woolwich, but was troubled afterwards I should say no further, being in a galley, lest he should think me too profuse in my journeys. The Comet appeared to-night, but duskishly. I went to bed, leaving my wife, and all her folks, and Will also, to come to make Christmas gambols to-night.

28*th.* My wife to bed at eight o'clock in the morning, which vexed me a little, but I believe there was no hurt in it at all, but only mirth.

[1] St. Dionis Backchurch.

Visited my Lady Sandwich, and was there, with
her and the young ladies, playing at cards till
night.   Then home **to bed, leaving my wife and
people up** to more sports, but without any great
satisfaction to myself.

30th.   To several places **to pay away** money,
to clear myself **in** all the world, and, among
others, **paid my** bookseller 6*l.* for books I had
from **him this day,** and the silversmith 22*l.* 18*s.*
for spoons, forks, and sugar-box.

31st.   To my accounts **of** the whole year till
past twelve at night, it being bitter cold, but yet
I was well satisfied with my work ; and, above
all, **to find myself, by the** great blessing of God,
worth **1349***l.***, by which, as I have spent very**
largely, so I have **laid** up above 500*l.* this year
above what **I** was worth this day twelve month.
The Lord make me for ever thankful to his holy
name **for it !**   Soon as ever **the** clock struck one,
I kissed my wife **in** the kitchen by the fireside,
wishing her a merry new year.   So ends the
old **year,** I bless God, with great joy to me, not
only from my having made **so good a** year of
profit, as having **spent** 420*l.* and laid up 540*l.*
and upwards : **but I bless God I** never have
been in so good plight as to my health in so very
cold weather as this is, nor indeed in any hot

weather, these ten years, as I am at this day,
and have been these four or five months. But
I am at a great loss to know whether it be my
hare's foot,[1] or taking every morning of a pill
of turpentine, or my having left off the wearing
of a gown. My family is my wife, in good
health, and happy with her; her woman Mercer, a pretty, modest, quiet maid; her chamber-
maid, Besse, her cook-maid Jane, the little girl
Susan, and my boy, which I have had about
half a year, Tom Edwards, which I took from
the King's Chapel; and as pretty and loving
quiet a family I have as any man in England.
My credit in the world and my office grows
daily, and I am in good esteem with everybody,
I think. My troubles of my uncle's estate
pretty well over; but it comes to be of little
profit to us, my father being much supported by
my purse. But great vexations remain upon
my father and me from my brother Tom's death
and ill condition, both to our disgrace and discontent, though no great reason for either.
Public matters are all in a hurry about a Dutch
war. Our preparations great; our provocations
against them great; and, after all our presump-
tion, we are now afraid as much of them as we

---

1 As a charm against the colic.

9

lately contemned them.   Everything else in
the State quiet, blessed be God!   My Lord
Sandwich at sea with the fleet, at Portsmouth;
sending some about to cruise for taking of
ships, which we have done to a great number.
This Christmas I judged it fit to look over all
my papers and books, and to tear all that I
found either boyish or not to be worth keeping,
or fit to be seen, if it should please God to take
me away suddenly."

A love of lucre seems to have shared a place
in Pepys's heart, with his fondness for dress
and good drink.   In fact, throughout the whole
Diary, he is mainly occupied with reckoning up
and securing his gains, — turning them into
good gold, — and bagging and hiding them in
holes and corners.   His prosperity, indeed, is
marvellous, and shows us how good a thing it
was to be in office, even two centuries ago.
There were evidently pretty pickings in the
Admiralty ; and the conscientious and cautious
Samuel does not appear to have been above receiving retainers and bribes in accordance with
the customs in vogue in those not over-scrupu-
lous days.   For instance, Pepys records, " I
met Captain Grove, who did give me a letter
addressed to myself from himself.   I discovered

money to be in it: and took it, knowing, as I found it to be, the proceed of the place I have got him to be, the taking up of vessels for Tangier. But I did not open it till I came home, not looking into it till all the money was out, that I might say I saw no money in the paper, if ever I should be questioned about it!"

In making up a year's balance, he says, with great satisfaction, that he has largely increased his wealth in the twelvemonth, and records an " abatement of outlay" for coats, bands, periwigs, &c.

The Dutch war stimulated the Secretary to very great exertions, as all the naval energies of the nation were necessarily called into action, and during the plague which ensued in the year 1665, when London was deserted, and the service almost completely abandoned, the whole management of the navy devolved upon him. Pepys behaved nobly during the existance of that terrible visitation, remaining at his post, regardless of the dangers which environed him, while others fled in dismay. "The sickness in general thickens around us, and particularly upon our neighborhood," observes the Secretary in writing to Sir William Coventry at this juncture. " You, sir, took your turn

of the sword, I must not therefore grudge to
take mine of the pestilence." To write a full
history of the mysterious malady, and a description of the fearful scenes it generated, was
reserved for a novelist of the next generation,
whose wonderful pen had the power of invest-
ing with an air of reality whatever it touched.
Pepys, writing to a friend, says, " The absence
of the court and the emptiness of the city takes
away all occasion of news, save only such
melancholy stories as would rather sadden than
find your Ladyship any divertisement in the
hearing: I have staid in the city till above
7400 died in one week, and of them about
6000 of the plague, and little noise heard day
nor night but tolling of bells : till I could walk
Lumberstreet, and not meet twenty persons
from one end to the other, and not fifty upon
the Exchange: till whole families (ten and
twelve together) have been swept away: till
my very physician (Dr. Burnet), who undertook to secure me against any infection (having
survived the month of his own being shut up),
died himself of the plague: till the nights
(though much lengthened) are grown too short
to conceal the burials of those who died the
day before, people being thereby constrained to

borrow daylight for service : lastly till I could neither find meat nor drink safe, the butchers being everywhere visited, my brewer's house shut up, and my baker with his whole family dead of the plague."

At this time comes news of the great victory gained over the Dutch fleet on the 3d of June. Says Pepys, " I to my Lord Treasurer's by appointment of Sir Thomas Ingrams to meet the Goldsmiths ; where I met with the great news at last newly come, brought by Bab May from the Duke of York, that we have totally routed the Dutch ; that the Duke himself, the Prince, my Lord Sandwich, and Mr. Coventry are all well ; which did put me into such joy, that I forgot almost all other thoughts. With great joy to the Cocke-pitt, where the Duke of Albemarle, like a man out of himself with content, new-told me all ; and by and by comes a letter from Mr. Coventry's own hand to him, which he never opened, which was a strange thing, but did give it me to open and read, and consider what was fit for our office to do in it, and leave the matter with Sir W. Clerke ; which, upon such a time and occasion, was a strange piece of indifference, hardly possible. I copied out the letter, and did also take min-

utes out of Sir W. Clerke's other letters; and
the sum of the news is : —

VICTORY OVER THE DUTCH, JUNE 3, 1665.[1]

This day they engaged : the Dutch neglecting
greatly the opportunity of the wind they had
of us ; by which they lost the benefit of their
fire-ships. The Earl of Falmouth, Muskerry,
and Mr. Richard Boyle [2] killed on board the
Duke's ship, the Royall Charles, with one shot :
their blood and brains flying in the Duke's
face ; and the head of Mr. Boyle striking down
the Duke, as some say. Earl of Marlborough,
Portland,[3] Rear Admiral Sansum,[4] to Prince
Rupert, killed, and Captain Kirby and Able-
son. Sir John Lawson wounded on the knee : [5]

---

[1] See Sir John Denham's Advice to a Painter concerning
the Dutch war, in Poems on State Affairs.

[2] Second son to the Earl of Burlington.

[3] Charles Weston, third Earl of Portland.

[4] " Robert Sansum, Commander of the Resolution, being
Rear-Admiral of the White."— Pepys's *Collection of Signs
Manual.*

[5] When Opdam's ship blew up, a shot from it mortally
wounded Sir John Lawson, which is thus alluded to in the
Poems on State Affairs : —

>   " —————— destiny allowed
> Him his revenge, to make his death more proud.
> A fatal bullet from his side did range,
> And battered Lawson; oh, too dear exchange !

hath had some bones taken out, and is likely to be well again. Upon receiving the hurt, he sent to the Duke for another to command the Royall Oake. The Duke sent Jordan[1] out of the St. George, who did brave things to her. Captain Jeremiah Smith, of the Mary, was second to the Duke, and stepped between him and Captain Seaton, of the Urania, 76 guns and 400 men, who had sworn to board the Duke; killed him 200 men, and took the ship; himself losing 99 men, and never an officer saved, but himself and lieutenant. His master indeed is saved, with his leg cut off. Admiral Opdam blown up, Trump killed, and said by

> He led our fleet that day too short a space,
> But lost his knee : since died, in glorious race :
> Lawson, whose valor beyond Fate did go,
> And still fights Opdam in the lake below."

In the same poem, Lord Falmouth's death is thus noticed : —

> " Falmouth was there, I know not what to act ;
> Some say 'twas to grow Duke, too, by contract.
> An untaught bullet, in his wanton scope,
> Dashes him all to pieces, and his Hope.
> Such was his rise, such was his fall, unpraised ;
> A chance-shot sooner took him than chance raised :
> His shattered head the fearless Duke distains,
> And gave the last first proof that he had brains."

[1] Afterwards Sir Joseph Jordan, Commander of the Royal Sovereign, and Vice-Admiral of the Red, 1672. He was knighted on the 1st July, 1665.

Holmes ; all the rest of their admirals, as they say, but Everson, whom they dare not trust for his affection to the Prince of Orange, are killed : we have taken and sunk, as is believed, about twenty-four of their best ships ; killed and taken near 8 or 10,000 men, and lost, we think, not above 700. A greater victory never known in the world. They are all fled ; some 43 got into the Texell, and others elsewhere, and we in pursuit of the rest. Thence, with my heart full of joy, home ; then to my Lady Pen's, where they are all joyed, and not a little puffed up at the good success of their father ; and good service indeed is said to have been done by him. Had a great bonfire at the gate ; and I, with my Lady Pen's people, and others, to Mrs. Turner's great room, and there down into the street. I did give the boys 4s. among them, and mighty merry : so home to bed, with my heart at great rest and quiet, saving that the consideration of the victory is too great for me presently to comprehend.

9th. To White Hall, and in my way met with Mr. Moore, who eases me in one point wherein I was troubled ; which was, that I heard of nothing said or done by my Lord Sandwich : but he tells me that Mr. Cooling,

my Lord Chamberlain's secretary, did hear the
King say that my Lord Sandwich had done
nobly and worthily.[1] The King, it seems, is
much troubled at the fall of my Lord Falmouth ;
but I do not meet with any man else that so
much as wishes him alive again, the world
conceiving him a man of too much pleasure to
do the King any good, or offer any good office
to him. But I hear, of all hands, he is confessed to be a man of great honor, that did
show it in this his going with the Duke, the
most that ever any man did. Home, where my
people busy to make ready a supper against
night for some guests, in lieu of my stone-feasts.
With my tailor to buy a silk suit, which though
I had one lately, yet I do, for joy of the good
news we have lately had of our victory over
the Dutch, which makes me willing to spare
myself something extraordinary in clothes ;
and, after long resolution of having nothing but
black, I did buy a colored silk ferrandin.

10*th*. In the evening home to supper ; and
there, to my great trouble, hear that the plague
is come into the City, though it hath, these
three or four weeks since its beginning, been

---

[1] See Charles II.'s letter of thanks to Lord Sandwich, in
Ellis's Letters.

wholly out of the City; but where should it
begin but in my good friend and neighbor's,
Dr. Burnett, in Fenchurch Street; which, in
both points, troubles me mightily.

11*th*. (Lord's Day.) Up, and expected long
a new suit; but, coming not, dressed myself in
my new black silk camelott suit; and, when
fully ready, comes my new one of colored ferrandin, which my wife puts me out of love
with, which vexes me. At noon, by invitation,
comes my two cousin Joyces and their wives —
my aunt James and he-cousin Harman — his
wife being ill. Had a good dinner for them,
and as merry as I could be in such company.
They being gone, I out of doors a little, to
show, forsooth, my new suit. I saw poor Dr.
Burnett's door shut; but he hath, I hear,
gained great good-will among his neighbors:
for he discovered it himself first, and caused
himself to be shut up of his own accord; which
was very handsome.

12*th*. Up, and in my yesterday's new suit to
the Duke of Albemarle, and thence returned;
and, with my tailor, bought some good lace for
my sleeve bands in Pater Noster Row. The
Duke of York is sent for last night, and expected to be here to-morrow."

In his Diary the Secretary has, of course, constant allusions to the terrible scourge which come in strangely, like the tones of a death-knell, among statements of every kind of gayety and dissipation ; for the plague did not do away with frivolity, nor with marrying and giving in marriage. We find him conversing with a friend, when they come close to a victim of the pestilence, who is being carried to " the silent house ; " and then follows this entry : ' Lord ! to see what custom is, that I am come to think nothing of it." Again : " To my office a little, and then to the Duke of Albemarle's about some business. The streets empty all the way, now, even in London, which is a sad sight. And to Westminster Hall, where talking, hearing very sad stories from Mrs. Mumford : among others, of Mr. Mitchell's son's family. And poor Will, that used to sell us ale at the Hall-door, his wife and three children died, all, I think, in a day. So home through the city again, wishing I may have no ill in going : but I will go, I think, no more thither." During the month of July, Pepys has a great deal to say about the wooing of his patron's daughter, Miss Jemimah Montagu, to whom we are first introduced in his Diary October 20, 1660. " All

other things well," says Samuel; "especially a
new interest I am making by a match in hand
between the eldest son of Sir G. Carteret and
Lady Jemimah Montagu." Our readers will
be amused with the story of the courtship,
which was in accordance with the old saw,
" Happy is the wooing that is not long a doing."

" *July* 14*th*. I by water to Sir G. Carteret's,
and there find my Lady Sandwich buying things
for my Lady Jem.'s wedding : and my Lady
Jem. is, beyond expectation, come to Dagenhams,[1] where Mr. Carteret is to go to visit
her to-morrow ; and my proposal of waiting
on him, he being to go alone to all persons
strangers to him, was well accepted, and so I
go with him. But, Lord ! to see how kind my
Lady Carteret is to her ! Sends her most rich

---

[1] Dagenhams, near Romford, the seat of Lady Wright,
widow of Sir Henry Wright, and sister of Lady Sandwich.
This estate was devised by Anne, daughter of Sir Henry and
Lady Wright, widow first of Sir Robert Pye, of Berkshire,
and afterwards of William Rider, Esq., only surviving child
of Sir Henry Wright, to her first cousin, Edward Carteret,
Postmaster-General, third son of Sir Philip Carteret and Lady
Jemimah Montagu, whose daughters, in 1749, sold it to Henry
Muilman : in 1772 it was again disposed of to Mr. Neave,
grandfather of the present proprietor (Sir Richard Digby
Neave, Bart.), who pulled down the old house built by Sir
Henry Wright, and erected the present mansion on a different
site. — See Lysons's *Environs.*

jewels, and provides bedding and things of all sorts most richly for her, which makes my Lady and me out of our wits almost to see the kindness she treats us all with, as if they would buy the young lady.

15*th.* Mr. Carteret and I to the ferry-place at Greenwich, and there staid an hour crossing the water to and again to get our coach and horses over; and by and by set out, and so toward Dagenhams. But, Lord! what silly discourse we had as to love-matters, he being the most awkward man ever I met with in my life as to that business. Thither we come, and by that time it began to be dark, and were kindly received by Lady Wright and my Lord Crewe. And to discourse they went, my Lord discoursing with him, asking of him questions of travel, which he answered well enough in a few words; but nothing to the lady from him at all. To supper, and after supper to talk again, he yet taking no notice of the lady. My Lord would have had me have consented to leaving the young people together to-night, to begin their amours, his staying being but to be little. But I advised against it, lest the lady might be too much surprised. So they led him up to his chamber, where I staid a little, to know how he liked the lady, which he told me he did mightily; but, Lord! in the dullest insipid manner that ever lover did. So I bid him good night, and down to prayers with my Lord Crewe's family: and, after prayers, my Lord, and Lady Wright, and I, to consult what to do; and it was agreed, at last, to have them go to church together, as the family used to do, though his lameness was a great objection against it. But, at last, my Lady Jem. sent me word by my Lady Wright, that it would be better to do just as they used to do before his coming; and therefore she desired to go to church, which was yielded to them.

16th. (Lord's Day.) I up, having lain with Mr. Moore in the chaplain's chamber. And, having trimmed myself, down to Mr. Carteret; and we walked in the gallery an hour or two, it being a most noble and pretty house that ever, for the bigness, I saw. Here I taught him what to do: to take the lady always by the hand to lead her, and telling him that I would find opportunity to leave them together, he should make these and these compliments, and also take a time to do the like to Lord Crewe and Lady Wright. After I had instructed him, which he thanked me for, owning that he needed

my teaching him, my Lord Crewe come down
and family, the young lady among the rest;
and so by coaches to church four miles off;
where a pretty good sermon, and a declaration
of penitence of a man that had undergone the
church's censure for his wicked life. Thence
back again by coach, Mr. Carteret having not
had the confidence to take his lady once by the
hand, coming or going, which I told him of
when we come home, and he will hereafter do
it. So to dinner. My Lord excellent discourse. Then to walk in the gallery, and to
sit down. By and by my Lady Wright and I
go out, and then my Lord Crewe, he not by
design, and lastly my Lady Crewe come out,
and left the young people together. And a
little pretty daughter of my Lady Wright's most
innocently come out afterwards, and shut the
door to, as if she had done it, poor child, by
inspiration: which made us without have good
sport to laugh at. They together an hour, and
by and by church-time, whither he led her into
the coach and into the church, where several
handsome ladies. But it was most extraordinary hot that ever I knew it. So home again,
and to walk in the gardens, where we left the
young couple a second time; and my Lady

Wright and I to walk together, who tells me that some new clothes must of necessity be made for Lady Jemimah, which and other things I took care of. Anon to supper, and excellent discourse and dispute between my Lord Crewe and the chaplain, who is a good scholar, but a nonconformist. Here this evening I spoke with Mrs. Carter, my old acquaintance, that hath lived with my Lady these twelve or thirteen years, the sum of all whose discourse and others for her is, that I would get her a good husband; which I have promised, but know not when I shall perform. After Mr. Carteret was carried to his chamber, we to prayers, and then to bed.

17*th*. Up all of us, and to billiards; my Lady Wright, Mr. Carteret, myself, and everybody. By and by, the young couple left together. Anon to dinner; and after dinner Mr. Carteret took my advice about giving to the servants 10*l*. among them, which he did, by leaving it to the chief man-servant, Mr. Medows, to do for him. Before we went, I took my Lady Jem. apart, and would know how she liked this gentleman, and whether she was under any difficulty concerning him. She blushed, and hid her face awhile; but at last I forced her to tell me. She answered, that she could readily obey what her father and mother had done; which was all she could say, or I expect. But, Lord! to see among other things, how all these great people here are afraid of London, being doubtful of anything that comes from thence, or that hath lately been there, that I was forced to say that I lived wholly at Woolwich. So anon took leave, and for London. In our way, Mr. Carteret did give me mighty thanks for my care and pains for him, and is mightily pleased, though the truth is, my Lady Jem. hath carried herself with mighty discretion and gravity, not being forward at all in any degree, but mighty serious in her answers to him, as by what he says and I observed, I collect. To Deptford, where mighty welcome, and brought the good news of all being pleased. Mighty mirth of my giving them an account of all; but the young man could not be got to say one word before me or my Lady Sandwich of his adventures; but, by what he afterwards related to his father and mother and sisters, he gives an account that pleases them mightily. Here Sir G. Carteret would have me lie all night, which I did most nobly, better than ever I did in my life; Sir G. Carteret being mighty kind to me, leading me to my chamber; and all their care now is,

10

to have the business ended ; and they have reason, because the sickness puts all out of order,
and they cannot safely stay where they are."

The day of the marriage — the 31st of
July — soon comes round. The doughty Diarist is in his glory, " being," he says, " in my
new colored silk vest and coat trimmed with
gold buttons, and gold broad lace round my
hands, very rich and fine." But we must give
Pepys's own complete narrative of the proceedings on this happy occasion.

" Up, and very betimes by six o'clock, at
Deptford, and there find Sir G. Carteret, and my
Lady ready to go : I being in my new-colored
silk suit, and coat trimmed with gold buttons,
and gold broad lace round my hands, very rich
and fine. By water to the Ferry, where, when
we come, no coach there ; and tide of ebb so
far spent as the horse-boat could not get off on
the other side of the river to bring away the
coach. So we were fain to stay there in the
unlucky Isle of Doggs, in a chilly place, the morning cool, and wind fresh, above two if not three
hours, to our great discontent. Yet, being upon
a pleasant errand, and seeing that it could not
be helped, we did bear it very patiently ; and it
was worth my observing to see how, upon these

two scores, **Sir G.** Carteret, the most passionate
man in the world, and that was in greatest haste
to be gone, did bear with it, and very pleasant
all the while, at least, not troubled so much as
to fret and storm at it. Anon the coach comes:
in the mean time, there coming a News thither
with his horse to go over, and told us he did
come from Islington this morning; and that
Proctor,[1] the vintner, of the Miter, in Wood
Street, and his son, are dead this morning there,
of the plague: he having laid out abundance of
money there, and was the greatest vintner for
some time in London for great entertainments.
We, fearing the canonical hour would be past
before we got thither, did, with a great deal of
unwillingness, send away the license and wed-
ding-ring. So that when we come, though we
drove hard with six horses, yet we found them
gone from home; and, going towards the church,
met them coming from church, which troubled
us. But, however, that trouble was soon over;
hearing it was well done: they being both in
their old clothes; my Lord Crewe giving her,
there being three coachfuls of them. The

---

[1] 1665, Aug. 1. Mr. Wm. Proctor, vintner, at yᵉ Mitre, in
Wood Street, with his young son, died at Islington (insol-
vent). *Ex peste.* — Smith's *Obituary.*

young lady, mighty sad, which troubled me ;
but yet I think is was only her gravity in a little
greater degree than usual.   All saluted her, but
I did not, till my Lady Sandwich did ask me
whether I saluted her or no.   So to dinner, and
very merry we were ; but in such a sober way
as never almost anything was in so great families : but it was much better.   After dinner,
company divided, some to cards, others to talk.
My Lady Sandwich and I up to settle accounts,
and pay her some money.   And mighty kind
she is to me, and would fain have had me gone
down for company with her to Hinchingbroke ;
but for my life I cannot.   At night to supper,
and so to talk ; and which, methought, was the
most extraordinary thing, all of us to prayers as
usual, and the young bride and bridegroom too :
and so, after prayers, soberly to bed ; only I
got into the bridegroom's chamber while he un-
dressed himself, and there was very merry, till
he was called to the bride's chamber, and into
bed they went.   I kissed the bride in bed, and
so the curtains drawn with the greatest gravity
that could be, and so good night.   But the
modesty and gravity of this business was so
decent, that it was to me indeed ten times more
delightful than if it had been twenty times more

merry and jovial. Whereas, I feared we must have sat up all night, we did here all get good beds, and I lay in the same I did before, with Mr. Brisband, who is a good scholar and sober man ; and we lay in bed, getting him to give me an account of Rome, which is the most delightful talk a man can have of any traveller : and so to sleep. Thus, I ended this month with the greatest joy that ever I did any in my life, because I have spent the greatest part of it with abundance of joy, and honor, and pleasant journeys, and brave entertainments, and without cost of money ; and at last live to see the business ended with great content on all sides."

During the months of August and September, the pestilence continued to make the most fearful ravages in London. The Diary records : —

" *Aug.* 10*th.* My she-cousin Porter, the turner's wife, to tell me that her husband was carried to the Tower, for buying of some of the King's powder, and would have my help, but I could give her none, not daring to appear in the business. By and by to the office, where we sat all the morning ; in great trouble to see the Bill this week rise so high, to above 4000 in all, and of them above 3000 of the plague. Home, to draw over anew my will, which I had bound

myself by oath to despatch by to-morrow night ;
the town growing so unhealthy, that a man
cannot depend upon living two days.

11*th.* To the Exchequer, about striking new
tallies, and I find the Exchequer, by proclamation, removing to Nonsuch.[1] Setting my house,
and all things, in the best order I can, lest it
should please God to take me away, or force
me to leave my house.

12*th.* Sent for by Sir G. Carteret, to meet
him and my Lord Hinchingbroke at Deptford,
but my Lord did not come thither, he having
crossed the river at Gravesend to Dagenhams,
whither I dare not follow him, they being afraid
of me ; but Sir G. Carteret says he is a most
sweet youth in every circumstance. Sir G.
Carteret being in haste of going to the Duke
of Albemarle and the Archbishop, he was pet-
tish. The people die so, that now it seems they
are fain to carry the dead to be buried by daylight, the nights not sufficing to do it in. And
my Lord Mayor commands people to be within
at nine at night all, as they say, that the sick
may have liberty to go abroad for air. There
is one also dead out of one of our ships at
Deptford, which troubles us mightily — the

---

[1] Nonsuch House, near Epsom.

Providence, fire-ship, which was just fitted to go to sea; but they tell me, to-day, no more sick on board. And this day W. Bodham tells me that one is dead at Woolwich, not far from the Ropeyard. I am told too, that a wife of one of the grooms at Court is dead at Salisbury; so that the King and Queen are speedily to be all gone to Wilton.[1] So God preserve us!

13*th*. (Lord's day.) It being very wet all day, clearing all matters, and giving instructions in writing to my executors, thereby perfecting the whole business of my will, to my very great joy; so that I shall be in much better state of soul, I hope, if it should please the Lord to call me away this sickly time. I find myself worth, besides Brampton estates, the sum of 2164*l*., for which the Lord be praised!

14*th*. To Sir G. Carteret; and, among other things, he told me, that he was not for the fanfaroone,[2] to make a show with a great title, as he might have had long since, but the main thing, to get an estate; and another thing, speaking of minding of business — ' By G—d,'

---

[1] Near Salisbury, then the seat of Philip, fifth Earl of Pembroke, who married Katharine, daughter of Sir Wm. Villiers, of Brookesby, cousin of the Duke of Buckingham.

[2] To make a great flourish or bravado. — *Cotgrave*.

says he, ' I will, and have already almost
brought it to that pass, that the King shall not
be able to whip a cat, but I mean to be at the
tail of it ! ' meaning, so necessary he is, and
the King and my Lord Treasurer all do confess
it, which, while I mind my business, is my own
case in this office of the Navy. After dinner,
beat Captain Cocke at billiards ; won about 8s.
of him and my Lord Brouncker. This night I
did present my wife with a diamond ring,
awhile since given me by Mr. Vines's brother,
for helping him to be a purser, valued at about
10l., the first thing of that nature I did give
her. Great fears we have that the plague will
be a great Bill this week.

15th. It was dark before I could get home,
and so land at Church-yard stairs, where, to my
great trouble, I met a dead corpse of the plague,
in the narrow alley, just bringing down a little
pair of stairs. But I thank God I was not
much disturbed at it. However, I shall beware
of being late abroad again.

16th. To the Exchange, where I have not
been a great while. But, Lord ! how sad a
sight it is to see the streets empty of people,
and very few upon the 'Change. Jealous of
every door that one sees shut up, lest it should

be the plague; and about us two shops in three, if not more, generally shut up. This day, I had the ill news from Dagenhams, that my poor Lord of Hinchingbroke his indisposition is turned to the small-pox. Poor gentleman! that he should be come from France so soon to fall sick, and of that disease too, when he should be gone to see a fine lady, his mistress! I am most heartily sorry for it.

18*th*. To Sheernesse, where we walked up and down, laying out the ground[1] to be taken in for a yard to lay provisions for cleaning and repairing of ships, and a most proper place it is for the purpose. Late in the dark to Gravesend, where great is the plague, and I troubled to stay there so long for the tide.

19*th*. Come letters from the King and Lord Arlington, for the removal of our office to Greenwich. I also wrote letters, and made myself ready to go to Sir G. Carteret, at Windsor; and, having borrowed a horse of Mr. Blackborough, sent him to wait for me at the Duke of Albemarle's door: when, on a sudden, a letter comes to us from the Duke of Albe-

---

[1] The yard and fortifications of Sheerness were designed and first " staked out " by Sir Barnard de Gomme. The original plan is in the British Museum.

marle, to tell us that the fleet is all come back to Solebay, and are presently to be despatched back again. Whereupon I presently by water to the Duke of Albemarle, to know what news; and there I saw a letter from my Lord Sandwich to the Duke of Albemarle, and also from Sir W. Coventry and Captain Teddiman; how my Lord having commanded Teddiman, with twenty-two ships, of which but fifteen could get thither, and of those fifteen but eight or nine could come up to play, to go to Bergen;[1] where, after several messages to and from the Governor of the Castle, urging that Teddiman ought not to come thither with more than five ships, and desiring time to think of it, all the while he suffering the Dutch ships to land their guns to the best advantage, Teddiman, on the second pretence, began to play at the Dutch ships, whereof ten East India-men, and in three hours' time, the town and castle, without any provocation, playing on our ships, they did cut all our cables, so as the wind being off the land, did force us to go out, and rendered our fire-ships useless, without doing anything, but what

[1] A view of this attack on Bergen, " described from the life in Aug., 1661, by C. H.," being a contemporary colored drawing, on vellum, showing the range of the ships engaged, is in the British Museum.

hurt of course our guns must have done them: we having lost five commanders, besides Mr. Edward Montagu[1] and Mr. Windham.[2] Our fleet is come home, to our great grief, with not above five weeks' dry and six days' wet provisions: however, must go out again; and the Duke hath ordered the Soveraigne,[3] and all other ships ready, to go out to the fleet, and strengthen them. * This news troubles us all, but cannot be helped. Having read all this news, and received commands of the Duke with great content, he giving me the words which, to my great joy, he hath several times said to me, that his greatest reliance is upon me; and my Lord Craven also did come

[1] Mr. Edward Montagu was killed in the action at Bergen, and is much lamented by his friends. — Earl of Arlington's *Letters.*

[2] This Mr. Windham had entered into a formal engagement, with the Earl of Rochester, " not without ceremonies of religion, that if either of them died, he should appear, and give the other notice of the future state, if there was any." He was probably one of the brothers of Sir Wm. Wyndham, Bart. See Wordsworth's *Ecclesiastical Biography.*

[3] " The Sovereign of the Seas " was built at Woolwich, in 1637, of timber which had been stripped of its bark, while growing in the spring, and not felled till the second autumn afterwards; and it is observed by Dr. Plot (*Phil. Trans.* for 1691), in his discourse on the most seasonable time for felling timber, written by the advice of Pepys, that after forty-seven years, " all the ancient timber then remaining in her, it was no easy matter to drive a nail into it." — *Quarterly Review.*

out to talk with me, and told me that I am in
mighty esteem with the Duke, for which I bless
God. Home ; and having given my fellow-officers an account hereof at Chatham, and wrote
other letters, I by water to Charing-Cross, to
the post-house, and there the people tell me they
are shut up ; and so I went to the new post-
house, and there got a guide and horses to
Hounslow. •So to Staines, and there, by this
time, it was dark night, and got a guide, who
lost his way in the forest, till. by help of the
moon, which recompenses me for all the pains
I ever took about studying of her motions, I
led my guide into the way back again ; and so
we made a man rise that kept a gate, and so he
carried us to Cranborne,[1] where, in the dark, I
perceive an old house new building, with a
great deal of rubbish, and was fain to go up a
ladder to . Sir G. Carteret's chamber. And
there, in his bed, I sat down, and told him all
my bad news, which troubled him mightily ;
but yet we were very merry, and made the best
of it ; and being myself weary, did take leave ;
and, after having spoken with Mr. Fenn[2]
in bed, I to bed in my Lady's chamber that she

[1] One of the Lodges belonging to the Crown in Windsor
Forest.
[2] Probably John Fenne of the Navy Office.

uses to lie in, where the Duchess of York, that now is, was born. So to sleep; being very well, but weary, and the better by having carried with me a bottle of strong water; whereof, now and then, a sip did me good.

20*th*. (Lord's Day.) Sir G. Carteret come and walked by my bedside half an hour, talking, and telling how my Lord is unblamable in all this ill success, he having followed orders; and that all ought to be imputed to the falseness of the King of Denmark, who, he told me as a secret, had promised to deliver up the Dutch ships to us; and we expected no less; and swears it will, and will easily, be the ruin of him and his kingdom, if we fall out with him, as we must in honor do; but that all that can be, must be to get the fleet out again, to intercept De Witt, who certainly will be coming home with the East India fleet, he being gone thither. I up, and to walk forth to see the place; and I find it to be a very noble seat in a noble forest, with the noblest prospect towards Windsor, and round about over many counties that can be desired; but otherwise a very melancholy place, and little variety, save only trees. So took horse for Staines, and thence to Branford, to Mr. Povy's. Mr. Povy not being at home, I lost my labor — only eat and drank there with his lady, and told my bad news, and hear the plague is round about them there. So away to Branford; and there, at the inn that goes down to the water-side, I 'light and paid off my post-horses, and so slipped on my shoes, and laid my things by, the tide not serving, and to church, where a dull sermon, and many Londoners. After church, to my inn, and eat and drank, and so about seven o'clock by water, and got, between nine and ten, to Queenhive, very dark; and I could not get my waterman to go elsewhere, for fear of the plague. Thence with a lantern, in great fear of meeting of dead corpses, carrying to be buried; but, blessed be God! met none, but did see now and then a link, which is the mark of them, at a distance.

Sept. 6th. To London, to pack up more things; and there I saw fires burning in the street, as it is through the whole City, by the Lord Mayor's order. Thence by water to the Duke of Albemarle's: all the way fires on each side of the Thames, and strange to see in broad daylight two or three burials upon the bankside, one at the very heels of another: doubtless, all of the plague; and yet at least forty or fifty people going along with every one of them. The Duke mighty pleasant with me; telling me that he is certainly informed that the Dutch were not come home upon the 1st instant, and so he hopes our fleet may meet with them.

7th. To the Tower, and there sent for the Weekly Bill, and find 8252 dead in all, and of them 6978 of the plague; which is a most dreadful number, and shows reasons to fear that the plague hath got that hold that it will yet continue among us. Thence to Branford, reading " The Villaine," a pretty good play, all the way. There a coach of Mr. Povy's [1] stood ready for me, and he at his house ready to come in, and so we together merrily to Swakely,[2] to Sir R. Viner's: a very pleasant place,

---

[1] Aug. 6, 1666. Dined with Mr. Povy, and then went with him to see a country-house he had bought near Brentford. — Evelyn's *Diary.*

[2] Swakeley House, in the parish of Ickenham, Middlesex, was built in 1638, by Sir Edmund Wright, whose daughter marrying Sir James Harrington, one of Charles I.'s judges, he became possessed of it *jure uxoris.* Sir Robert Vyner, Bart., to whom the property was sold in 1665, entertained Charles II. at Guildhall, when Lord Mayor. The house was lately the residence of Thomas Clarke, Esq., whose father, in 1750, bought the estate of Mr. Lethieullier, to whom it had been alienated by the Vyner family. — Lysons's *Environs.* Sir Robert Vyner was ruined by the shutting of the Exchequer. The crown owed him on 1st January, 1676, no less a sum than 416,724*l.* 13*s.* 1*d.*, to pay which, the King granted him

bought by him of Sir James Harrington's lady. He took us up and down with great respect, and showed us all his house and grounds; and it is a place not very modern in the garden nor house, but the most uniform in all that ever I saw; and some things to excess. Pretty to see over the screen of the hall, put up by Sir J. Harrington, a long Parliament-man, the King's head, and my Lord of Essex [1] on one side, and Fairfax on the other; and, upon the other side of the screen, the parson of the parish, and the lord of the manor and his sisters. The window-cases, door-cases, and chimneys of all the house are marble. He showed me a black boy that he had, that died of a consumption; and, being dead, he caused him to be dried in an oven, and lies there entire in a box. By and by to dinner, where his lady [2] I find yet

25,000*l.* 9*s.* 4*d.*, per annum, out of the duty of Excise. These particulars are stated by Lord Keeper Somers, in his judgment, delivered in the Exchequer Chamber. In the *Spectator* (No. 462) is told the story of Sir Robert's successfully urging the King, at an entertainment given by him, "to return and take t'other bottle." Vyner afterwards erected a statue of the Merry Monarch in Stock's Market, and rendered the Crown many great services.

[1] The Parliament General.

[2] Mary, daughter of John Whitchurch, Esq., and widow of Sir Thomas Hyde, Bart., of Albury, Herts.

handsome, but hath been a very handsome woman : now is old. Hath brought him near 100,000*l.*, and now he lives, no man in England in greater plenty, and commands both King and Council with his credit he gives them. After dinner, Sir Robert led us up to his long gallery, very fine, above stairs, and better, or such, furniture I never did see. A most pleasant journey we had back. Povy tells me, by a letter he showed me, that the King is not, nor hath been of late, very well, but quite out of humor ; and, as some think, in a consumption, and weary of everything. He showed me my Lord Arlington's house [1] that he was born in, in a town called Harlington : and so carried me through a most pleasant country to Branford, and there put me into my boat, and good night. So I wrapped myself warm, and by water, got to Woolwich, about one in the morning.

November 24th. To London, and there, in

---

[1] Dawley House, near Hounslow, long the seat of the Bennet family. Harlington, in which parish it is situated, gave the title of Baron and Earl to Sir Henry Bennet ; the aspirate being dropped (it may be said, " according to the custom of London "). The mansion was alienated by Ford Grey, Earl of Tankerville, to Viscount Bolingbroke, since which it has often changed owners.

my way, at my old oyster shop in Gracious Street, bought two barrels of my fine woman of the shop, who is alive after all the plague, which now is the first observation or inquiry we make at London concerning everybody we know. To the 'Change, where very busy with several people, and mightily glad to see the 'Change so full, and hopes of another abatement still the next week. I went home with Sir G. Smith to dinner, sending for one of my barrels of oysters, which were good, though come from Colchester, where the plague hath been so much. Here a very brave dinner, though no invitation; and, Lord! to see how I am treated, that come from so mean a beginning, is matter of wonder to me. But it is God's mercy to me, and his blessing upon my taking pains, and being punctual in my dealings. Visited Mr. Evelyn, where most excellent discourse with him; among other things, he showed me a ledger [1] of a Treasurer of the Navy, his great grandfather, just 100 years old; which I seemed mighty fond of, and he did present me with it, which I take as a great rarity; and he hopes to find me more, older

---

[1] This ledger is now in the British Museum, amongst some of Pepys's Papers, in the Ducket Collection.

than it. He also showed us several letters of the old Lord of Leicester's,[1] in Queen Elizabeth's time, under the very handwriting of Queen Elizabeth, and **Queen Mary**, Queen of **Scots** ; and others, very venerable names. But, Lord ! how poorly, methinks, **they wrote** in those days, **and** in what **plain uncut paper**.

26*th.* (Lord's Day.) **Up** before day to dress myself to go toward Erith, which I would do by land, it being a horrible cold frost to go by water : so borrowed **two horses of** Mr. Howell and his friend, and with much ado set out, after my horses being frosted,[2] which **I know not** what it means to this day, and my boy having lost one **of my spurs and stockings**, carrying them to the smith's, and I borrowed a stocking, and so got up, and Mr. **Tooker with** me, and rode to Erith, and there on **board my Lord Brouncker** met with **Sir W. Warren** upon his business, among others, and did a great deal ; **Sir J. Minnes, as God would have it**, not being there to hinder us with his impertinencies. To

---

[1] Amongst these documents, still in the Pepysian Library, — for Evelyn complains that he lent them to Pepys, who omitted to return them, — are some letters relating to the death of Amy Robsart, Lady Robert Dudley.

[2] Frosting means, having the horse's shoes turned up by the smith.

my wife at Woolwich, where I found, as I had
directed, a good dinner to be made against to-
morrow, and invited guests in the yard, meaning to be merry, in order to her taking leave,
for she intends to come in a day or two to me
for altogether.   But here, they tell me, one of
the houses behind them is infected, and I was
fain to stand there a great while, to have their
back-doors opened, but they could not, having
locked them fast, against any passing through,
so was forced to pass by them again, close to
their sick beds, which they were removing out
of the house, which troubled me: so I made
them uninvite their guests, and to resolve of
coming all away to me to-morrow.

December 25*th*. (Christmas Day.) To church
in the morning, and there saw a wedding in the
church, which I have not seen many a day ;
and the young people so merry one with
another! and strange to see what delight we
married people have to see these poor fools de-
coyed into our condition, every man and woman
gazing and smiling at them.   Here I saw again
my beauty Lethulier.   Home to look over and
settle my papers, both of my accounts private,
and those of Tangier, which I have let go so
long that it were impossible for any soul, had I

died, to understand them, or ever come to good end in them. I hope God will never suffer me to come to that disorder again.

26th. To the office, where Sir John Minnes and my Lord Brouncker and I met, to give our directions to the Commanders of all the ships in the river to bring in lists of their ships' companies, where young Seymour, among 20 that stood bare, stood with his hat on — a proud, saucy young man. To Mr. Cuttle's, being invited, and dined nobly and neatly; with a very pretty house and a fine turret at top, with winding stairs, and the first prospect I know about all Greenwich, save the top of the hill. Saw some fine writing-work and flourishing of Mr. Hoare, with one that I knew long ago, an acquaintance of Mr. Tomson's at Westminster, that is this man's clerk. It is the story of the several Archbishops of Canterbury, engrossed in vellum, to hang up in Canterbury Cathedral in tables, in lieu of the old ones, which are almost worn out.

27th. Home to my wife, and angry about her desiring a maid yet, before the plague is quite over. It seems Mercer is troubled that she hath not one under her, but I will not venture my family by increasing it, before it is safe.

30th. All the afternoon to my accounts; and there find myself, to my great joy, a great deal worth, above 4000*l.*, for which the Lord be praised! and is principally occasioned by my getting 500*l.* of Cocke, for my profit in his bargains of prize goods, and from Mr. Gauden's making me a present of 500*l.* more, when I paid him 800*l.* for Tangier.

31st. (Lord's Day.) Thus ends this year, to my great joy, in this manner. I have raised my estate from 1300*l.* in this year to 4400*l.* I have got myself greater interest, I think, by my diligence, and my employments increased by that of Treasurer for Tangier and Surveyor of the Victuals. It is true we have gone through great melancholy because of the great plague, and I put to great charges by it, by keeping my family long at Woolwich; and myself and another part of my family, my clerks, at my charge, at Greenwich, and a maid at London; but I hope the King will give us some satisfaction for that. But now the plague is abated almost to nothing, and I intending to get to London as fast as I can. The Dutch war goes on very ill, by reason of lack of money; having none to hope for, all being put into disorder by a new Act that is made as an experiment to bring credit to the Exchequer, for goods and money to be advanced upon the credit of that Act. The great evil of this year, and the only one indeed, is the fall of my Lord Sandwich, whose mistake about the prizes hath undone him, I believe, as to interest at Court; though sent, for a little palliating it, Embassador into Spain, which he is now fitting himself for. But the Duke of Albemarle goes with the Prince to sea this next year, and my Lord is very meanly spoken of; and, indeed, his miscarriage about the prize goods is not to be excused, to suffer a company of rogues to go away with ten times as much as himself, and the blame of all to be deservedly laid upon him. My whole family hath been well all this while, and all my friends I know of, saving my aunt Bell, who is dead, and some children of my cousin Sarah's, of the plague. But many of such, as I know very well, dead; yet, to our great joy, the town fills apace, and shops begin to be open again. Pray God continue the plague's decrease! for that keeps the Court away from the place of business, and so all goes to rack as to public matters, they at this distance not thinking of it.

January 1st, 1666. Called up by five o'clock by Mr. Tooker, who wrote, while I dictated to him, my business of the Pursers; and so, without eating or drinking, till three in the afternoon, to my great content, finished it.[1]

2d. Up by candle-light again, and my business being done, to my Lord Brouncker's, and there find Sir J. Minnes and all his company, and Mr. Boreman and Mrs. Turner, but, above all, my dear Mrs. Knipp, with whom I sang, and in perfect pleasure I was to hear her sing, and especially her little Scotch song of 'Barbary Allen;' and to make our mirth the completer, Sir J. Minnes was in the highest pitch of mirth, and his mimical tricks, that ever I saw, and most excellent pleasant company he is, and the best musique that ever I saw, and certainly would have made an excellent actor, and now would be an excellent teacher of actors. Then, it being past night, against my will, took leave.

3d. I to the Duke of Albemarle and back again: and, at the Duke's, with great joy, I

---

1 This document is in the British Museum, and is entitled, "A Letter from Mr. Pepys, dated at Greenwich, 1 January, 1665–6, which he calls his New Year's Gift to his honorable friend, Sir William Coventry, wherein he lays down a method for securing his Majesty in husbandly execution of the Victualling Part of the Naval Expense." It consists of nineteen closely written folio pages, and is a remarkable specimen of Pepys's business habits.

received the good news of the decrease of the
plague this week to 70, and but 253 in all ;
which is the least Bill hath been known these
twenty years in the city, though the want of
people in London is it, that must make it so
low, below the ordinary number for Bills. So
home, and find all my good company I had bespoke, as Coleman and his wife, and Laneare,
Knipp and her surly husband ; and good music
we had, and among other things, Mr. Coleman
sang my words I set, of ' Beauty, retire,' and
they praise it mightily. Then to dancing and
supper, and mighty merry till Mr. Rolt come
in, whose pain of the toothache made him no
company, and spoilt ours ; so he away, and
then my wife's teeth fell of aching, and she to
bed. So forced to break up all with a good
song, and so to bed.

5*th.* I with my Lord Brouncker and Mrs.
Williams by coach with four horses to London,
to my Lord's house in Covent Garden.[1] But,
Lord ! what staring to see a nobleman's coach
come to town ! And porters everywhere bow
to us ; and such begging of beggars ! And
delightful it is to see the town full of people

---

[1] In the Piazza ; and one of the largest houses in what was
then the most fashionable part of London.

again; and shops begin to open, though in
many places seven or eight together, and more,
all shut; but yet the town is full, compared to
what it used to be.   I mean the City end; for
Covent Garden and Westminster are yet very
empty of people, no Court nor gentry being
there.   Home, thinking to get Mrs. Knipp, but
could not, she being busy with company, but
sent me a pleasant letter, writing herself, 'Barbary Allen.'   Reading a discourse about the
river of Thames, the reason of its being choked
up in several places with shelfs: which is
plain, is by the encroachments made upon the
River, and running out of causeways into the
River, at every wood-wharf: which was not
heretofore, when Westminster Hall and White
Hall were built, and Hedriffe Church, which
now are sometimes overflown with water.

6th. To a great dinner and much company.
Mr. Cuttle and his lady and I went, hoping to
get Mrs. Knipp to us, having wrote a letter to
her in the morning, calling myself 'Dapper
Dicky'[1] in answer to hers of 'Barbary Allen,'
but could not, and am told by the boy that carried my letter, that he found her crying; and I

---

[1] A song called "Dapper Dicky" is in the British Museum;
it begins, "In a barren tree." It was printed in 1710.

fear she lives a sad life with that ill-natured
fellow her husband; so we had a great, but I a
melancholy dinner. After dinner to cards, and
then comes notice that my wife is come unex-
pectedly to me to town: so I to her. It is only
to see what I do, and why I come not home;
and she is in the right that I would have a little more of Mrs. Knipp's company before I go
away. My wife to fetch away my things from
Woolwich, and I back to cards, and after cards
to choose King and Queen, and a good cake
there was, but no marks found; but I privately
found the clove, the mark of the knave, and
privately put it into Captain Cocke's piece,
which made some mirth, because of his lately
being known by his buying of clove and mace
of the East India prizes. At night home to my
lodging, where I find my wife returned with
my things. It being Twelfth Night, they had
got the fiddler, and mighty merry they were;
and I above, come not to them, leaving them
dancing, and choosing King and Queen."

During the great fire of London, September,
1666, respecting which there are many curious
details in the Diary, Pepys rendered the most
essential service by sending up the artificers
from the dock-yards, who adopted the plan of

blowing up houses, and in that way ultimately
arrested the progress of the flames.

"*September 6th.* Up about five o'clock, and
met Mr. Gauden at the gate of the office, I
intending to go out, as I used, every now and
then, to-day, to see how the fire is, to call our
men to Bishop's-gate, where no fire had yet
been near, and there is now one broke out:
which did give great grounds to people, and to
me too, to think that there is some kind of plot
in this, on which many by this time have been
taken, and it hath been dangerous for any
stranger to walk in the streets, but I went with
the men, and we did put it out in a little time;
so that that was well again. It was pretty to
see how hard the women did work in the ken-
nels, sweeping of water; but then they would
scold for drink, and be as drunk as devils. I
saw good butts of sugar broke open in the
street, and people give and take handfuls out,
and put into beer, and drink it. And now all
being pretty well, I took boat, and over to
Southwarke, and took boat on the other side
the bridge, and so to Westminster, thinking to
shift myself, being all in dirt from top to bottom; but could not there find any place to buy
a shirt or a pair of gloves, Westminster Hall

being full of people's goods, those in Westminster having removed all their goods, and the Exchequer money put into vessels to carry to Nonsuch;[1] but to the Swan, and there was trimmed: and then to White Hall, but saw nobody; and so home. A sad sight to see how the river looks: no houses nor church near it, to the Temple, where it stopped. At home, did go with Sir W. Batten, and our neighbor, Knightly, who, with one more, was the only man of any fashion left in all the neighborhood thereabouts, they all removing their goods, and leaving their houses to the mercy of the fire; to Sir R. Ford's, and there dined in an earthen platter — a fried breast of mutton; a great many of us, but very merry, and indeed as good a meal, though as ugly a one, as ever I had in my life. Thence down to Deptford, and there with great satisfaction landed all my goods at Sir G. Carteret's safe, and nothing missed I could see or hear. This being done to my great content, I home, and to Sir W. Batten's, and there, with Sir R. Ford, Mr. Knightly, and one Withers, a professed lying rogue, supped well, and mighty merry, and our

---

[1] At which house the Exchequer had been kept during the plague.

fears over.   From them to the office, and there
slept with the office full of laborers, who talked,
and slept, and walked all night long there.   But
strange it is to see Clothworkers' Hall on fire
these three days and nights in one body of
flame, it being the cellar full of oil.

7*th.*   Up by five o'clock ; and blessed be God !
find all well ; and by water to Pane's Wharf.[1]
Walked thence, and saw all the town burned,
and a miserable sight of Paul's church, with all
the roofs fallen, and the body of the quire fallen
into St. Fayth's ; Paul's school also, Ludgate
and Fleet Street.   My father's house, and the
church, and a good part of the Temple the like.
So to Creed's lodging, near the New Exchange,
and there find him laid down upon a bed ; the
house all unfurnished, there being fears of the
fire's coming to them.   There borrowed a shirt
of him, and washed.   To Sir W. Coventry at
St. James's, who lay without curtains, having
removed all his goods ; as the King at White
Hall, and every body had done, and was doing.
He hopes we shall have no public distractions
upon this fire, which is what everybody fears,
because of the talk of the French having a
hand in it.   And it is a proper time for discon-

---

[1] Paul's Wharf.

tents; but all men's minds are full of care to protect themselves and save their goods: the Militia is in arms everywhere. Our fleets, he tells me, have been in sight one of another, and most unhappily, by foul weather were parted, to our great loss, as in reason they do conclude; the Dutch being come out only to make a show, and please their people; but in very bad condition as to stores, victuals, and men. They are at Boulogne, and our fleet come to St. Ellen's. We have got nothing, but have lost one ship, but he knows not what. Thence to the Swan, and there drank; and so home, and find all well. My Lord Brouncker, at Sir W. Batten's, tells us the General [1] is sent for up, to come to advise with the King about business at this juncture, and to keep all quiet; which is great honor to him, but I am sure is but a piece of dissimulation. So home, and did give orders for my house to be made clean; and then down to Woolwich, and there find all well. Dined, and Mrs. Markham come to see my wife. This day our Merchants first met at Gresham College, which, by proclamation, is to be their Exchange. Strange to hear what is bid for houses all up and down here; a friend of Sir

---

[1] The Duke of Albemarle.

W. Rider's having 150*l.* for what he used to let
for 40*l.* per annum.   Much dispute where the
Custom House shall be ; thereby the growth of
the City again to be foreseen.   My Lord Treasurer, they say, and others, would have it at the
other end of the town.   I home late to Sir W.
Penn's, who did give me a bed, but without curtains or hangings, all being down.   So here I
went the first time into a naked bed, only my
drawers on ; and did sleep pretty well : but still
both sleeping and waking had a fear of fire in
my heart, that I took little rest.   People do all
the world over cry out of the simplicity of my
Lord Mayor in general ; and more particularly
in this business of the fire, laying it all upon
him.   A proclamation is come out for markets
to be kept at Leaden-hall and Mile-end Greene,
and several other places about the town ; and
Tower Hill and all churches to be set open to
receive poor people.

November 9th.   To Mrs. Pierce's by appointment, where we find good company : a fair lady,
my Lady Prettyman,[1] Mrs. Corbet,[2] Knipp, and

---

[1] Margaret, daughter and heir of Sir Matthew Mennes, K. B.,
and wife of Sir John Prettyman, Bart., M. P. for Leicester.

[2] There was an actress of this name.   She played Cleoly, at
the King's House, in Edward Howard's " Man of New-
market," 1678.

for men, Captain Downing, **Mr. Lloyd,** Sir W.
Coventry's clerk, and one Mr. Tripp, who dances
well. After our first bout of dancing, Knipp
and **I** to sing, and Mercer and Captain Downing, who loves and understands music, would
by all means have **my song** of ' Beauty, retire :' which Knipp had spread abroad, and he
extols it above anything he ever heard. **Going**
to dance again, and then comes news that White
Hall was **on fire** ; and presently more particulars, that the Horse-guard was on fire ;[1] and so
we run up to the garret, and find it so ; a horrid
great fire ; and by and by we saw and heard
part of it blown up with powder. The ladies
begun presently to be afraid : one fell into fits.
The whole town in an alarm. Drums beat and
trumpets, and the Horse-guards every where
spread, running up and down in the street. And

[1] " November 9th. Between seven and eight at night,
there happened a fire in the Horse Guard House, in the Tilt
Yard, over against Whitehall, which at first arising, it is
supposed, from some snuff of a candle falling amongst the
straw, broke out with so sudden a flame, that at once it seized
the north-west part of that building ; but being so close under
His Majesty's own eye, it was, by the timely help His Majesty
and His Royal Highness caused to be applied, immediately
stopped, and by ten o'clock wholly mastered, with the loss
only of that part of the building it had at first seized."— *The
London Gazette,* No. 103.

I begun to have mighty apprehensions how
things might be, for we are in expectation from
common fame, this night, or to-morrow, to have
a massacre, by the having so many fires one
after another, as that in the City, and at same
time begun in Westminster, by the Palace, but
put out ; and since in Southwarke, to the burning down some houses ; and now this do make
all people conclude there is something extraordinary in it ; but nobody knows what.   By
and by comes news that the fire is slackened ;
so then we were a little cheered up again, and
to supper, and pretty merry.   But, above all,
there comes in the dumb boy that I knew in
Oliver's time, who is mightily acquainted here,
and with Downing ; and he made strange signs
of the fire, and how the King was abroad, and
many things they understood, but I could not,
which I wondered at ; and discoursing with
Downing about it, 'Why,' says he, 'it is only
a little use, and you will understand him, and
make him understand you with as much ease
as may be.'   So I prayed him to tell him that
I was afraid that my coach would be gone, and
that he should go down and steal one of the
seats out of the coach and keep it, and that

would make the coachman to stay. He did this, so that the dumb boy did go down, and, like a cunning rogue, went into the coach, pretending to sleep; and, by and by, fell to his work, but finds the seats nailed to the coach. So he could not do it; however, staid there, and staid the coach till the coachman's patience was quite spent, and beat the dumb boy by force, and so went away. So the dumb boy came up, and told him all the story, which they below did see all that passed, and knew it to be true. After supper, another dance or two, and then news that the fire is as great as ever, which puts us all to our wits'-end; and I mightily anxious to go home, but the coach being gone, and it being about ten at night, and rainy, dirty weather, I knew not what to do, but to walk out with Mr. Batelier, myself resolving to go home on foot, and leave the women there. And so did; but at the Savoy got a coach, and come back and took up the women; and so, having, by people come from the fire, understood that the fire was overcome and all well, we merrily parted, and home. Stopped by several guards and constables quite through the town, round the wall, as we went, all being in arms. Being come home, we to cards, till two in the morning, and drinking lamb's-wool.[1] So to bed.

December 25*th*. (**Christmas Day.**) Lay pretty long in bed, and then rose, leaving my wife desirous to sleep, having sat up till four this morning seeing her maids make mince-pies.   I to church, where our parson Mills made a good sermon. Then home, and dined well on some good ribs of beef roasted, and mince-pies ; only my wife, brother, and Barker, and plenty of good wine of my own, and my heart full of true joy ; and thanks to God Almighty for the goodness of my condition at this day.   After dinner, I begun to teach my wife and Barker my song, ' It is decreed,' which pleases me mightily.   Walked alone on foot to the Temple, thinking to have seen a play all alone ; but there, missing of any bills, concluded there was none, and so back home ; and there with my brother reducing the names of all my books to an alphabet, and then to supper and to bed.

26*th*. To the Duke's house, to a play.   It was indifferently done, Gosnell not singing, but a new wench, that sings naughtily.   Thence home, and there Mr. Andrews to the viol, who

---

[1] A beverage made of ale, mixed with sugar, nutmeg, and the pulp of roasted apples.

plays most excellently on it. Thence to dance, here being Pembleton **come**, by my wife's **direction**, and a fiddler; and we got, also, the elder Batelier to-night, and Nan Wright, and mighty merry we were, and danced; and so till twelve at night, and **to** supper, and then to cross **purposes**, mighty merry, and then to bed."

Our annalist, as the observant reader **must have** noticed, was a constant and critical *habitué* of the theatre. A week is seldom allowed to pass without his witnessing a play, with which he is often dissatisfied and " ill pleased ;" but, after a careful study of his Diary, **we have** failed to discover that the sturdy Briton **of the** seventeenth century was addicted to **expressing** his displeasure in such an emphatic manner as prevailed among members of Congress in the **days** of Andrew Jackson, *videlicet* — shooting at the actors. Here is **the record of one of** those terrible dramatic critics : The Hon. James Blair, **M. C.** from South Carolina, attended the Washington theatre **one** evening in March, 1834, when, the players displeasing him, **he** drew his pistol and **fired at the actors on the** stage, the **bullet** passing just **above the head of** Miss Jefferson, daughter of **Joe Jefferson, Sen.** The players stampeded **from the stage, and a**

quick curtain was run down. Presently the
manager appeared, looking pale and agitated,
and said to the audience, "Ladies and gentlemen, if there is to be shooting at the actors on
the stage, it will be impossible for the per-
formance to go on!"

Our next citation, and the first segregated
from the year 1667, is concerning a duel and
another matter, being a part of Pepys's record
for July 29th. . . . "Cousin Roger and Creed
to dinner with me, and very merry: but among
other things they told me of the strange, bold
sermon of Dr. Creeton yesterday, before the
King; how he preached against the sins of the
Court, and particularly against adultery; over
and over instancing how for that single sin in
David, the whole nation was undone; and of
our negligence in having our castles without
ammunition and powder when the Dutch came
upon us; and how we have no courage nowa-
days, but let our ships be taken out of our har-
bor. Here Creed did tell us the story of the duel
last night, in Covent-garden, between Sir H. Bellassis and Tom Porter. It is worth remembering the silliness of the quarrel, and is a kind of
emblem of the general complexion of this whole
kingdom at present. They two dined yesterday

at Sir **Robert Carr's**,[1] where it seems people do
drink high, all that come. It happened that
these two, the greatest friends in the world,
were talking together: and Sir H. Bellassis
talked a little louder than ordinary to Tom
Porter, giving of him some advice. Some of
the company standing by said, 'What! are
they quarrelling, that they talk so high?' Sir
H. Bellassis, hearing it, said, 'No!' says he:
'I would have you know I never quarrel, but
I strike; and take that as a rule of mine!'
'How?' says Tom Porter, 'strike! I would
I could see the man in England that durst give
me a blow!' With that Sir H. Bellassis did
give him a box of the ear; and so they were
going to fight there, but were hindered. And
by and by Tom Porter went out; and meeting
Dryden the poet, told him of the business, and
that he was resolved to fight Sir H. Bellassis
presently; for he knew, if he did not, they
should be friends to-morrow, and then the blow
would rest upon him; which he would prevent,
and desired Dryden to let him have his boy to
bring him notice which way Sir H. Bellassis
goes. By and by he is informed that Sir H.

---

[1] Baronet, of Sleaford, Lincolnshire, and one of the pro-
posed Knights of the Royal Oak for that county.

Bellassis' coach was coming: so Tom Porter went out of the Coffee-house where he staid for the tidings, and stopped the coach, and bade Sir H. Bellassis come out. 'Why,' says H. Bellassis, 'you will not hurt me coming out, will you?'—'No,' says Tom Porter. So out he went, and both drew: and H. Bellassis having drawn and flung away his scabbard, Tom Porter asked him whether he was ready? The other answering him he was, they fell to fight, some of their acquaintance by. They wounded one another, and H. Bellassis so much that it is feared he will die: and finding himself severely wounded, he called to Tom Porter, and kissed him, and bade him shift for himself; 'for,' says he, 'Tom, thou hast hurt me; but I will make shift to stand upon my legs till thou mayest withdraw, and the world not take notice of you, for I would not have thee troubled for what thou hast done.' And so whether he did fly or no I cannot tell; but Tom Porter showed H. Bellassis that he was wounded too: and they are both ill, but H. Bellassis to fear of life. And this is a fine example; and H. Bellassis a Parliament-man,[1] too, and both of them extraordinary friends! . . . Cousin Roger did acquaint

---

[1] He was serving for Grimsby.

me in private with an offer made of his marrying of Mrs. Elizabeth Wiles, whom I know ; a kinswoman of Mr. Honiwood's, an ugly old maid, but good housewife, and is said to have 2500*l.* to her portion ; but if I can find that she has but 2000*l.*, which he prays me to examine, he says he will have her, she being one he had long known intimately, and a good housewife, and discreet woman ; though I am against it in my heart, she being not handsome at all : and it hath been the very bad fortune of the Pepyses that ever I knew, never to marry an handsome woman, excepting Ned Pepys." [1]

On the 22d of January, 1668, Pepys goes with my Lord Brouncker to dine at Sir D. Gauden's, where " a good dinner and much good company, and a fine house, and especially two rooms very fine, he hath built there. His lady a good lady : but my Lord led himself and me to a great absurdity in kissing all the ladies, but the first of all the company, leaving her out — I know not how ; and I was loath to do it since he omitted it." On the last day of the same month, he records, " It is observed, and is true,

[1] Edward Pepys, of Broomsthorpe, who married Elizabeth Walpole. The author's own wife could not be included amongst the plain women whom the Pepyses married? — it is otherwise well for his domestic peace that he wrote in cipher.

in the late fire of London, that the fire burned
just as many parish-churches as there were
hours from the beginning to the end of the
fire: and next, that there were just as many
churches left standing as there were taverns left
standing in the rest of the City that was not
burned, being, I think, thirteen in all of each,
which is pretty to observe.

February 1st. To the office till past two
o'clock, where at the Board some high words
passed between Sir W. Penn and I, begun by
me, and yielded to by him, I being in the right
in finding fault with him for his neglect of duty.
Home, my head mighty full of business now on
my hands, viz., of finishing my Tangier Accounts; of auditing my last year's Accounts;
of preparing answers to the Commissioners of
Accounts; of drawing up several important letters to the Duke of York and the Commissioners
of the Treasury; the marrying of my sister;
the building of a coach and stables against summer, and the setting many things in the office
right; and the drawing up a new form of Con-
tract with the Victualler of the Navy, and several other things, which pains, however, will go
through with.

2d. (Lord's Day.) All the morning set-

ting my books in order in my presses, for the
following year, their number being much increased since the last, so as I am fain to lay by
several books to make room for better, being
resolved to keep no more than just my presses
will contain. A very good dinner we had, of a
powdered leg of pork and a loin of lamb roasted.

3*d.* To the Duke of York's house, to the
play, " The Tempest," which we have often
seen, and particularly this day I took pleasure
to learn the time of the seaman's dance.

4*th.* To Kate Joyce's, where the jury did
sit where they did before, about her husband's
death, and their verdict put off for fourteen
days longer, at the suit of somebody, under
pretence of the King; but it is only to get
money out of her to compound the matter.
But the truth is, something they will make out
of Stillingfleete's sermon, which may trouble us,
he declaring, like a fool, in his pulpit, that he
did confess that his losses in the world did make
him do what he did. This vexes me to see how
foolish our Protestant Divines are, while the
Papists do make it the duty of Confessor to be
secret, or else nobody would confess their sins
to them. All being put off for to-day, I took
my leave of Kate, who is mightily troubled at

it for her estate sake, not for her husband ; for
her sorrow for that, I perceive, is all over.

5*th*.   To the Commissioners of Accounts,
where I was called in, and did take an oath to
declare the truth to what they should ask me,
which is a great power, I doubt more than the
Act do, or as some say can, give them, to force
a man to swear against himself; and so they
fell to inquire about the business of prize-goods,
wherein I did answer them as well as I could,
in everything the just truth, keeping myself to
them.   I do perceive, at last, that that they do
lay most like a fault to me was, that I did buy
goods upon my Lord Sandwich's declaring that
it was with the King's allowance, and my be-
lieving it, without seeing the King's allowance,
which is a thing I will own, and doubt not to
justify myself in.   But what vexed me most
was, their having some watermen by, to witness
my saying that they were rogues that had betrayed my goods, which was upon some discontent with one of the watermen that I employed at
Greenwich, who I did think did discover the goods
sent from Rochester to the Custom-House officer ;
but this can do me no great harm.   They were
inquisitive into the minutest particulars, and had
had great information ; but I think that they can

do me no hurt — at the worst, more than to make
me refund, if it must be known, what profit I
did make of my agreement with Captain Cocke;
and yet, though this be all, I do find so poor a
spirit within me, that it makes me almost out
of my wits, and puts me to so much pain, that
I cannot think of anything, nor do anything but
vex and fret, and imagine myself undone.
After they had done with me, they called in
Captain Cocke, with whom they were shorter;
and I do fear he may answer foolishly; but I
hope to preserve myself, and let him shift for
himself as well as he can. Mr. Cooke come
for my Lady Sandwich's plate, which I must
part with, and so endanger the losing of my
money, which I lent upon my thoughts of securing myself by that plate. But it is no great
sum — but 60*l.*: and if it must be lost, better
that, than a greater sum. I away back again,
to find a dinner anywhere else, and so I, first,
to the Ship Tavern, thereby to get a sight of
the pretty mistress of the house, with whom I
am not yet acquainted at all, and I do always
find her scolding, and do believe she is an ill-
natured devil, that I have no great desire to
speak to her. Mr. Moore mightily commends my
Lord Hinchingbroke's match and Lady, though

he buys her 10,000*l.* dear, by the jointure and
settlement his father makes her; and says that
the Duke of York and Duchess of York did
come to see them in bed together, on their
wedding-night, and how my Lord had fifty
pieces of gold taken out of his pocket that
night, after he was in bed. He tells me that
an Act of Comprehension is likely to pass this
Parliament, for admitting of all persuasions in
religion to the public observation of their particular worship, but in certain places, and the
persons therein concerned to be listed of this, or
that Church; which, it is thought, will do them
more hurt than good, and make them not own
their persuasion. He tells me that there
is a pardon passed to the Duke of Buckingham, and my Lord of Shrewsbury, and
the rest, for the late duel and murder;[1] which
he thinks a worse fault than any ill use my late

[1] The Royal pardon was thus announced in the *Gazette* of
February 24, 1668: "This day his Majesty was pleased to
declare at the Board, that whereas, in contemplation of the
eminent services heretofore done to his Majesty by most of
the persons who were engaged in the late duel or rencontre,
wherein William Jenkins was killed, he doth graciously pardon the said offence: nevertheless, He is resolved from hence-
forth that on no pretence whatsoever any pardon shall be
hereafter granted to any person whatsoever for killing of any
man, in any duel or rencontre, but that the course of law shall
wholly take place in all such cases."

Lord Chancellor ever put the **Great Seal** to, and will be so thought by the Parliament, for them to be pardoned without bringing them to any trial : and that my Lord **Privy-Seal** therefore would not have it pass his hand, but made it go by immediate warrant ; or at least they knew that he would not pass it, and so did direct it to go by immediate warrant, that it might not come to him. He tells me what a character my Lord Sandwich hath sent over of Mr. Godolphin, as the worthiest man, and such a friend to him as he may be trusted in anything relating to him in the world ; as one from whom, he says, he hath infallible assurances that he will remain his friend ; which is very high, but indeed they say the gentleman is a fine man.

6th. Sir H. Cholmly tells me how the Parliament, which is to meet again to-day, are likely to fall heavy on the business of the Duke of Buckingham's pardon ; and I shall be glad of it : and that the King hath put out of the Court the two Hides,[1] my Lord Chancellor's two sons, and also the Bishops of Rochester[2] and Winchester,[3] the latter of whom should have

---

[1] Lord Cornbury and Laurence Hyde .
[2] John Dolben, afterwards Archbishop of York.
[3] George Morley.

preached before him yesterday, being Ash-
Wednesday, and had his sermon ready, but was
put by; which is great news. My wife being
gone before, I to the Duke of York's playhouse;
where a new play of Etheredge's,[1] called 'She
Would if she Could;' and though I was there
by two o'clock, there was 1000 people put back
that could not have room in the pit; and I at
last, because my wife was there, made shift to
get into the 18*d.* box, and there saw; but,
Lord! how full was the house, and how silly
the play, there being nothing in the world good
in it, and few people pleased in it. The King
was there; but I sat mightily behind, and could
see but little, and hear not all. The play being
done, I into the pit to look for my wife, it
being dark and raining, but could not find her;
and so staid going between the two doors and
through the pit an hour and a half, I think,
after the play was done; the people staying
there till the rain was over, and to talk with
one another. And, among the rest, here was
the Duke of Buckingham to-day openly sat in

---

[1] Sir George Etherege, the celebrated wit and dramatic
writer. He is said to have died in France, subsequently to
the Revolution, having followed the fortunes of his royal
master, James II.

the pit; and there I found him with my Lord Buckhurst, and Sedley, and Etheredge, the poet; the last of whom I did hear mightily find fault with the actors, that they were out of humor, and had not their parts perfect,[1] and that Harris did do nothing, nor could so much as sing a ketch in it; and so was mightily concerned: while all the rest did, through the whole pit, blame the play as a silly, dull thing, though there was something very roguish and witty; but the design of the play, and end, mighty insipid. At last I did find my wife; and with her was Betty Turner, Mercer, and Deb. So I got a coach, and a humor took us, and I carried them to Hercules Pillars, and there did give them a kind of a supper of about 7s., and very merry, and home round the town, not through the ruins: and it was pretty how the coachman by mistake drives us into the ruins from London-wall into Coleman Street: and would persuade me that I lived there. And the truth is, I did think that he and the linkman had contrived some roguery; but it proved only a mistake of the coachman; but it was a cunning

---

[1] Shadwell confirms this complaint of Etherege's in the Preface to his own *Humorists.* Harris played Sir Josceline Jolly.

place to have done us a mischief in, as any I know, to drive us out of the road into the ruins, and there stop, while nobody could be called to help us. But we come safe home.

7th. Met my cousin, Roger Pepys, the Parliament meeting yesterday and adjourned to Monday next; and here he tells me that Mr. Jackson, my sister's servant,[1] is come to town, and hath this day suffered a recovery on his estate, in order to the making her a settlement. There is a great trial between my Lord Gerard and Carr to-day, who is indicted for his life at the King's Bench, for running from his colors; but all do say that my Lord Gerard, though he designs the ruin of this man, will not get anything by it. To the Commissioners of Accounts, and there presented my books, and was made to sit down, and used with much respect, otherwise than the other day, when I come to them as a criminal about the business of prizes. I sat here with them a great while, while my books were inventoried. I find these gentlemen to sit all day, and only eat a bit of bread at noon, and a glass of wine; and are resolved to go through their business with great severity and method. Met by cousin Roger again, and Mr.

---

[1] *i. e.,* suitor.

Jackson, who is a plain young man, handsome enough for Pall, one of no education nor discourse, but of few words, and one altogether that, I think, will please me well enough. My cousin had got me to give the odd sixth 100*l.* presently, which I intended to keep to the birth of the first child : and let it go — I shall be eased of the care. So there parted, my mind pretty well satisfied with this plain fellow for my sister, though I shall, I see, have no pleasure nor content in him, as if he had been a man of reading and parts, like Cumberland. Lord Brouncker, and W. Pen, and I, and with us Sir Arnold Breames, to the King's playhouse, and there saw a piece of 'Love in a Maze,' a dull, silly play, I think ; and after the play, home with W. Pen and his son Lowther, whom we met there.

9th. Cousin Roger and Jackson by appointment come to dine with me, and Creed, and very merry, only Jackson hath few words, and I like him never the worse for it. The great talk is of Carr's coming off in all his trials, to the disgrace of my Lord Gerard, to that degree, and the ripping up of so many notorious roguerics and cheats of my Lord's, that my Lord, it is thought, will be ruined ; and, above all, do

show the madness of the House of Commons,
who rejected the petition of this poor man by a
combination of a few in the House ; and, much
more, the base proceedings, just the epitome of
all our public managements in this age, of the
House of Lords, that ordered him to stand in
the pillory for those very things, without hearing and examining what he hath now, by the
seeking of my Lord Gerard himself, cleared
himself of, in open Court, to the gaining himself the pity of all the world, and shame forever to my Lord Gerard. To the Strand, to
my bookseller's, and there bought an idle roguish French book, which I have bought in plain
binding, avoiding the buying of it better bound,
because I resolve, as soon as I have read it, to
burn it, that it may not stand in the list of
books, nor among them, to disgrace them if it
should be found. My wife well pleased with
my sister's match, and designing how to be
merry at their marriage."

One of the most characteristic, and at the
same time creditable pieces of *naïvete* that we
meet with in Samuel's journal, is the account
he gives of the tremendous success of an orator-
ical broadside which he delivered at the bar of
the House of Commons some two months after

the date of our last extract, in explanation and defence of alleged mismanagements in the navy, a subject then under discussion in that assembly. Parliament probably knew very little about the business, and no one, probably, was so well informed as Pepys ; and this, doubtless, was the great merit of his discourse, and the secret of his success. Willing as we are to give the Secretary credit for industry, clearness, and good judgment, we think it perfectly evident from his manner of writing, and from the fact of his subsequent obscurity in Parliament, that he could never have had any pretensions to the character of an orator. Be that as it may, the effort gave singular satisfaction to its worthy author : " Vexed and sickish to bed, and there slept about three hours, and then waked, and never in so much trouble in all my life, thinking of the task I have upon me, and upon what dissatisfactory grounds, and what the issue of it may be to me." This passage occurs in his Diary, March 4. The following day he says, —

" *5th*. With these thoughts I lay troubling myself till six o'clock, restless, and at last getting my wife to talk to me to comfort me, which she at last did, and made me resolve to quit my hands of this Office, and endure the trouble no longer than I can clear myself of it. So with great trouble, but yet with some ease, from the discourse with my wife, I up, and at my Office, whither come my clerks, and I did huddle the best I could some more notes for my discourse to-day, and by nine o'clock was ready, and did go down to the Old Swan, and there by boat, with T. Harvey and W. Hewer with me, to Westminster, where I found myself come time enough, and my brethren all ready. But I full of thoughts and trouble touching the issue of this day ; and, to comfort myself, did go to the Dog and drink half-a-pint of mulled sack, and in the Hall [Westmister] did drink a dram of brandy at Mrs. Hewlett's ; and with the warmth of this did find myself in better order as to courage, truly. So we all up to the lobby ; and between eleven or twelve o'clock, were called in, with the mace before us, into the House, where a mighty full House ; and we stood at the bar, namely, Brouncker, Sir J. Minnes, Sir T. Harvey, and myself, W. Pen being in the House, as a member. I perceive the whole House was full of expectation of our defence what it would be, and with great prejudice. After the Speaker had told us the dissatisfaction of the House, and read the Report of the Committee, I began our defence most acceptably and smoothly, and continued at it without any hesitation or loss, but with full scope, and all my reason free about me, as if it had been at my own table, from that time till past three in the afternoon; and so ended, without any interruption from the Speaker; but we withdrew. And there all my Fellow-Officers, and all the world that was within hearing, did congratulate me, and cry up my speech as the best thing they ever heard; and my Fellow-Officers were overjoyed in it; and we were called in again by and by to answer only one question, touching our paying tickets to ticket-mongers; and so out; and we were in hopes to have had a vote this day in our favor, and so the generality of the House was; but my speech, being so long, many had gone out to dinner and come in again half drunk; and then there are two or three that are professed enemies to us and everybody else; among others, Sir T. Littleton, Sir Thomas Lee,[1] Mr. Wiles, the coxcomb whom I saw heretofore at the cock-fighting, and few others; I say, these did rise up and speak against the coming to a vote now, the House not being full, by reason of several being at

[1] Of Hartwell, Bucks; created a Baronet 1660.

dinner, but most because that the House was to
attend the King this afternoon, about the business of religion, wherein they pray him to put
in force all the laws against Nonconformists and
Papists ; and this prevented it, so that they put
it off to to-morrow come se'nnight.   However,
it is plain we have got great ground ; and everybody says I have got the most honor that any
could have had opportunity of getting ; and
so our hearts mightily overjoyed at this success.
We all to dinner to my Lord Brouncker's —
that is to say, myself, T. Harvey, and W. Pen,
and there dined ; and thence to Sir Anthony
Morgan, who is an acquaintance of Brouncker's,
a very wise man : we after dinner to the King's
house, and there saw part of 'The Discontented Colonel.'   To my wife, whom W. Hewer
had told of my success, and she overjoyed ; and,
after talking awhile, I betimes to bed, having
had no quiet rest a good while.

6*th*.   Up betimes, and with Sir D. Gauden to
Sir W. Coventry's chamber : where the first
words he said to me was, " Good-morrow, Mr.
Pepys, that must be Speaker of the Parliament-
house : " and did protest I had got honor forever in Parliament.   He said that his brother,[1]

---

[1] Henry Coventry.

that sat **by** him, **admires** me ; and another gentleman **said that I** could not get less than **1000l.**
a-year if I would put on a gown and plead at
the Chancery-bar ; but, what pleases me most,
he tells me that the Solicitor-General[1] did protest that he thought I spoke the best of any man
in England.   After several talks with him alone,
touching his own businesses, he carried me to
White Hall, and there parted ; and I to the
Duke of York's lodgings, and find him going to
the Park, it being a very fine morning, and I
after him ; and as soon as he saw me, he told
me, with great satisfaction, that I had converted a great many yesterday, and did, with great
praise of me, go on with the discourse with me.
And, by and by, overtaking the King, the King
and Duke of York came to me both ; and he[2]
said, ' Mr. Pepys, I am very glad of your success yesterday ; ' and fell to talk of my well
speaking ; **and** many of the Lords there.   My
Lord Barkeley did cry me up for what they had
heard of it ; and others, Parliament-men there,
about the King, did say that they never heard **such**
a speech in their lives delivered in that manner.
Progers, of the Bedchamber, swore to me after-

[1] Sir Heneage Finch.
[2] The King.

wards before Brouncker, in the afternoon, that
he did tell the King that he thought I might
match the Solicitor-General. Everybody that
saw me almost came to me, as Joseph Williamson and others, with such eulogies as cannot be
expressed. From thence I went to Westminster Hall, where I met Mr. G. Montagu, who
came to me and kissed me, and told me that he
had often heretofore kissed my hands, but now
he would kiss my lips: protesting that I was
another Cicero, and said, all the world said the
same of me. Mr. Ashburnham, and every
creature I met there of the Parliament, or that
knew anything of the Parliament's actings, did
salute me with this honor: — Mr. Godolphin;
— Mr. Sands, who swore he would go twenty
miles, at any time, to hear the like again, and
that he never saw so many sit four hours
together to hear any man in his life, as there
did to hear me; Mr. Chichly, — Sir John Dun-
comb, — and everybody do say that the kingdom will ring of my abilities, and that I have
done myself right for my whole life: and so
Captain Cocke, and others of my friends, say
that no man had ever such an opportunity of
making his abilities known; and, that I may
cite all at once, Mr. Lieutenant of the Tower

did tell me that Mr. Vaughan did protest to
him, and that in his hearing, he said so to the
Duke of Albemarle, and afterwards to Sir W.
Coventry, that he had sat twenty-six years in
Parliament and never heard such a speech there
before; for which the Lord God make me
thankful! and that I may make use of it not to
pride and vain-glory, but that, now I have this
esteem, I may do nothing that may lessen it! I
spent the morning thus walking in the Hall,
being complimented by everybody with admiration: and at noon stepped into the Legg with
Sir William Warren, who was in the Hall, and
there talked about a little of his business, and
thence into the Hall a little more, and so with
him by coach as far as the Temple almost, and
there 'light, to follow my Lord Brouncker's
coach, which I spied, and so to Madam Williams's, where I overtook him, and agreed upon
meeting this afternoon. To White Hall, to
wait on the Duke of York, where he again and
all the company magnified me, and several in
the Gallery: among others, my Lord Gerard,
who never knew me before nor spoke to me, desires his being better acquainted with me; 'and
[said] that, at table where he was, he never
heard so much said of any man as of me, in his

whole life. So waited on the Duke of York,
and thence into the Gallery, where the House
of Lords waited the King's coming out of the
Park, which he did by and by; and there, in
the Vane-room, my Lord Keeper delivered a
message to the King, the Lords being about
him, wherein the Barons of England, from
many good arguments very well expressed in
the part he read out of, do demand precedence
in England of all noblemen of either of the
King's other two kingdoms, be their title what
it will; and did show that they were in England reputed but as Commoners, and sat in the
House of Commons, and at conferences with
the Lords did stand bare. It was mighty worth
my hearing: but the King did only say that he
would consider of it, and so dismissed them.[1]
Thence, with the Lieutenant of the Tower, in
his coach home; and there, with great pleasure,
with my wife, talking and playing at cards a little — she, and I, and W. Hewer, and Deb.

7th. Mercer, my wife, Deb., and I, to the
King's playhouse, and there saw "The Spanish
Gipseys,"[2] the second time of acting, and the

[1] The point of precedence was settled by the Act of Union.
They have rank next after the peers of the like degree in England at the time of the Union.

[2] "The Spanish Gipsie," a comedy, by T. Middleton and W.
Rowley.

first I saw it. A very silly play, only great variety of dances, and those most excellently done, especially one part by one Hanes,[1] only lately come thither from the Nursery, an understanding fellow, but yet, they say, hath spent 1000*l.* a-year before he come thither. This day my wife and I full of thoughts about Mrs. Pierce's sending me word that she, and my old company, Harris and Knipp, would come and dine with us next Wednesday, how we should do — to receive or put them off, my head being, at this time, so full of business, and my wife in no mind to have them neither, and yet I desire it.

8th. (Lord's Day.) To White Hall, where met with very many people still that did congratulate my speech the other day in the House of

---

[1] The famous **Joseph Haynes**, who was so popular, that two biographies of him were printed in 1701, after his death. One of them, entitled *The Life of the famous Comedian Jo. Haynes, containing his Comical Exploits and Adventures, both at Home and Abroad,* 8vo, states that he had acted under Captain Bedford, " whilst the playhouse in Hatton Garden lasted." This must have been the " Nursery " here alluded to by Pepys. Haynes was the first actor on record who delivered a prologue sitting on an ass. He was soon afterwards followed in his folly by Pinkethman; and by **Liston**, in our day. Haynes seems to have been a low comedian, and a capital dancer. One dramatic piece is attributed to him, " A Fatal Mistake," 4to, 1692.

Commons, and I find all the world almost rings
of it. With Sir W. Coventry, who I find full
of care in his own business, how to defend himself
against those that have a mind to choke him ;
and though, I believe, not for honor and for the
keeping his employment, but for safety and reputation's sake, is desirous to preserve himself
free from blame.   He desires me to get information against Captain Tatnell, thereby to
diminish his testimony, who, it seems, hath a
mind to do W. Coventry hurt : and I will do it
with all my heart ; for Tatnell is a very rogue.
He would be glad, too, that I could find anything proper for his taking notice against Sir F.
Hollis.   To dinner with Sir G. Carteret to
Lincoln's Inn Fields, where I find mighty deal
of company — a solemn day for some of his
and her friends, and dine in the great dining-
room above stairs, where Sir G. Carteret himself, and I, and his son, at a little table, the
great table being full of strangers.   Here my
Lady Jem. do promise to come and bring my
Lord Hinchingbroke and his Lady some day
this week, to dinner to me, which I am glad of.
After dinner, I up with her husband, Sir Philip
Carteret, to his closet, where, beyond expectation, I do find many pretty things, wherein he

appears to be ingenious, such as in painting,
and drawing, and making of watches, and such
kind of things, above my expectation; though,
when all is done, he is a sneak, who owns his
owing me 10*l.* for his lady two or three years
ago, and yet cannot provide to pay me.[1]

9th. By coach to White Hall, and there met
Lord Brouncker: and he and I to the Commissioners of the Treasury, where I find them
mighty kind to me, more, I think, than was
wont. And here I also met Colvill, the goldsmith: who tells me, with great joy, how the
world upon the 'Change talks of me; and how
several Parliament-men, viz., Boscawen[2] and
Major [Lionel] Walden, of Huntingdon, who,
it seems, do deal with him, do say how bravely
I did speak, and that the House was ready to
have given me thanks for it: but that, I think,
is a vanity."

A few days later, Pepys is informed, to his
inexpressible satisfaction, that the Speaker says
he never heard such a defence made in all his
life in the House, and that "the Solicitor-
General do commend me even to envy." On

---

[1] He entered the theatre upon credit.

[2] Edward Boscaewen, M. P. for Truro, ancestor of the present Viscount Falmouth.

the 13th, the happy Secretary meets my Lady
Hinchingbroke, "and she mighty civil: and
with my Lady Jemimah do resolve to be very
merry to-morrow at my house. My Lady
Hinchingbroke I cannot say is a beauty, nor
ugly: but is altogether a comely lady enough,
and seems very good-humored. Thence home;
and there find one laying of my napkins against
to-morrow in figures of all sorts: which is
mighty pretty: and it seems it is his trade, and
he gets much money by it." Our next extract
shows how curiously some words have changed
their signification in the two hundred years
that have elapsed since Pepys wrote. "This
morning my wife did, with great pleasure, show
me her stock of jewels, increased by the ring
she hath made lately as my Valentine's gift this
year, a Turky stone set with diamonds: and
with this, and what she had, she reckons that
she hath above 150l. worth of jewels of one
kind or other; and I am glad of it, for it is
fit the wretch should have something to content
herself with." The fashionable wives of the
year of our Lord 1867 would not take it very
complacently if their liege lords were to desig-
nate them as "wretches;" nor would they be
well pleased to be fobbed off with a beggarly

seven hundred and fifty dollars worth of jewelry, when at least a dozen fair denizens of the good city of Gotham have diamonds alone to the value of one hundred thousand dollars. A few days later, Pepys goes to the theatre. "I was prettily served this day at the play-house door : where giving six shillings into the fellow's hand for three of us, the fellow by legerdemain did convey one away, and with so much grace faced me down that I did give him but five, that, though I knew the contrary, yet I was overpowered by his so grave and serious demanding the other shilling that I could not deny him, but was forced by myself to give it him." March 20, we have this entry : "Thence home, and there in favor to my eyes staid at home, reading the ridiculous History of my Lord Newcastle,[1] wrote by his wife : which shows her to be a mad, conceited, ridiculous woman, and he an ass to suffer her to write what she writes to him and of him. So to bed, my eyes being very bad : and I know not how in the world to abstain from reading." Again he says, " With my wife to the King's House

---

[1] A copy of this work was lately sold at an auction sale for $230. Charles Lamb alludes to it in one of the charming Essays of Elia.

14

to see 'The Virgin Martyr,'[1] the first time it
hath been acted in a great while : and it is
mighty pleasant : not that the play is worth
much, but it is finely acted by Beck Marshall.
But that which did please me beyond anything
in the whole world, was the wind musique when
the angel comes down ; which is so served that
it ravished me, and indeed, in a word, did
wrap up my soul so that it made me really
sick, just as I have formerly been when in love
with my wife : that neither then, nor all the
evening going home, and at home, I was able
to think of anything, but remained all night
transported, so as I could not believe that ever
any musique hath that real command over the
soul of a man as this did upon me : and makes
me resolve to practise wind musique and to
make my wife do the like.

August 31, 1668. To the Duke of York's
play-house, and saw 'Hamlet,' which we have
not seen this year before or more ; and mightily
pleased with it, but above all with Betterton,
the best part, I believe, that ever man acted.

September 3. To my bookseller's for 'Hobbs'
Leviathan,' which is now mightily called for :
and what was heretofore sold for 8s. I now give

---

[1] A tragedy, by Philip Massinger.

14s. at the second hand, and is sold for 30s., it being a book the Bishops will not let be printed again.

4th. To the fair to see the play ' Bartholomew-fair,' with puppets. And it is an excellent play : the more I see it the more I love the wit of it : only the business of abusing the Puritans begins to grow stale and of no use, they being the people that at last will be found the wisest. . . .

23d. At noon comes Mr. Evelyn to me about some business with the Office, and there in discourse tells me of his loss to the value of 500*l.* which he hath met with in a late attempt of making bricks upon an adventure with others, by which he presumed [expected] to have got a great deal of money: [on which the shrewd Samuel comments], so that I see the most ingenious men may sometimes be mistaken."

On the 3d of December, Pepys records, " Home to dinner, and then abroad again with my wife to the Duke of York's play-house, and saw ' The Unfortunate Lovers,'[1] a mean play I think, but some parts very good, and excellently acted. We sat under the boxes, and saw the fine ladies : among others, my Lady Kerneguy,

---

[1] A tragedy by Sir William Davenant.

who is most devilishly painted.   And so home,
it being mighty pleasure to be alone with my
poor wife in a coach of our own to a play, and
makes us appear mighty great, I think, in the
world : at least, greater than ever I could, or
my friends for me, have once expected : or, I
think, than ever any of my family ever yet
lived in my memory, but my cousin Pepys in
Salisbury Court."

Our next citation from the curious and quaint
Diary records a domestic infelicity, and Samuel
naïvely confesses that Mrs. Pepys was very
near acting on the legend of St. Dunstan, who,

> "———— as the story goes,
> Once pulled the devil by the nose
> With *red-hot tongs*, which made him roar,
> That he was heard three miles or more."

"*Jan.* 12, 1669. . . . This evening I observed
my wife mighty dull, and I myself was not
mighty fond, because of some hard words she
did give me at noon, out of a jealousy at my
being abroad this morning, which God knows,
it was upon the business of the Office unex-
pectedly : but I to bed, not thinking but she
would come after me.   But waking by and by,
out of a slumber, which I usually fall into presently after my coming into the bed, I found she

did not prepare to come to bed, but got fresh candles, and more wood for her fire, it being mighty cold, too. At this being troubled, I after awhile prayed her to come to bed; so, after an hour or two, she silent, and I now and then praying her to come to bed, she fell out into a fury, that I was a rogue, and false to her. I did, as I might truly, deny it, and was mightily troubled, but all would not serve. At last, about one o'clock, she come to my side of the bed, and drew my curtain open, and with the tongs red hot at the ends, made as if she did design to pinch me with them, at which, in dismay, I rose up, and with a few words she laid them down; and did by little and little, very sillily, let all the discourse fall; and about two, but with much seeming difficulty, come to bed, and there lay well all night, and long in bed talking together, with much pleasure, it being, I know, nothing but her doubt of my going out yesterday, without telling her of my going, which did vex her, poor wretch! last night, and I cannot blame her jealousy, though it do vex me to the heart.

March 4th. . . . And so I parted,[1] with great

---

[1] From Sir William Coventry in the Tower, sent there for challenging the **Duke of Buckingham.**

content, that I had so earlily seen him there;
and so going out, did meet Sir Jer. Smith going
to meet me, who had newly been with Sir W.
Coventry. And so he and I by water to Redriffe, and so walked to Deptford, where I have
not been, I think, these twelve months: and
there to the Treasurer's house,[1] where the
Duke of York is, and his Duchess; and there
we find them at dinner in the great room,
unhung; and there was with them my Lady
Duchess of Monmouth, the Countess of Falmouth, Castlemaine, Henrietta Hide [2] (my
Lady Hinchinbroke's sister), and my Lady
Peterborough. And after dinner Sir Jer.
Smith and I were invited down to dinner with
some of the Maids of Honor, namely, Mrs.
Ogle,[3] Blake,[4] and Howard,[5] which did me good

[1] See it marked in the Plan of Deptford, in Evelyn's Diary.
[2] Henrietta, fifth daughter to the Earl of Burlington, married Lawrence Hyde, afterwards created Earl of Rochester.
[3] Anne Ogle, daughter of Thomas Ogle, of Pinchbeck, in
Lincolnshire. She was afterwards the first wife of Craven
Howard (son of Mrs. Howard), brother of her fellow-maid
of honor. — See Evelyn's *Diary.*
[4] Margaret Blagge, or Blague, daughter of Colonel Blague,
and afterwards wife of Sidney Godolphin. Her Life, written
by Evelyn, needs only to be mentioned here.
[5] Dorothy, the elder daughter of Mrs. Howard. She afterwards married Colonel James Graham, of Levens, Keeper of
the Privy Purse of the Duke of York. Their daughter, Kath-

to have the honor to dine with, and look on
them; and the Mother of the Maids,[1] and Mrs.
Howard,[2] the mother of the Maid of Honor of
that name, and the Duke's housekeeper here.
Here was also Monsieur Blancfort,[3] Sir Richard
Powell,[4] Colonel Villiers,[5] Sir Jonathan Tre-

arine Graham, married her cousin, Henry Bowes Howard,
fourth Earl of Berkshire and eleventh Earl of Suffolk.

[1] The *mother of the maids* in the Court of Queen Katharine
was Bridget, Lady Sanderson, daughter of Sir Edward Tyr-
rell, Knt., and wife of Sir William Sanderson, Gentleman of
the Privy Chamber. It is possible, however, that some one
filled the like office in the household of the Duchess of York.

[2] Elizabeth, daughter of Lowthiel, Lord Dundas, wife of
William Howard, fourth son of the first Earl of Berkshire.
Her son, Craven Howard, married, first, Anne Ogle, men-
tioned above; and, secondly, Mary, daughter of George
Bower, of Elford in Staffordshire, by whom he had Henry
Bowes Howard, who married Katharine Graham. It was by
means of Mrs. Howard, who, as housekeeper to the Duke of
York, resided in the Treasurer's house at Deptford, that
Evelyn, who lived at Sayes Court, adjoining the Royal Yard,
first became acquainted with Mrs. Godolphin, and it is to
Lady Sylvius, the younger daughter of Mrs. Howard, that he
addresses her Life.

[3] In 1677 he succeeded to the titles and estates of his father-
in-law, Sir George Sondes, who, in April, 1676, was created
Earl of Feversham and Viscount Sondes. As Earl of Feversham, Blancfort became of great importance during the short
but eventful reign of James II. He died in 1709.

[4] Sir Richard Powle, of Shottesbrooke, Berks, Master of
the Horse to the Duchess of York.

[5] Edward Villiers, Master of the Robes, and Groom of the
Bedchamber to the Duke of York. He was afterwards
knighted, and is the direct ancestor of the Earls of Jersey.

lawny,[1] and others. And here drank most excellent, and great variety, and plenty of wines,
more than I have drank, at once, these seven
years, but yet did me no great hurt. Having
dined very merrily, and understanding by
Blancfort how angry the Duke of York was,
about their offering to send Saville to the Gate-
house among the rogues; and then, observing
how this company, both the ladies and all, are
of a gang, and did drink a health to the union
of the two brothers, and talking of others as
their enemies, they parted, and so we up; and
there I did find the Duke of York and Duchess,
with all the great ladies, sitting upon a carpet,
on the ground, there being no chairs, playing
at ' I love my love with an A, because he is so
and so : and I hate him with an A, because of
this and that :' and some of them, but particularly the Duchess herself, and my Lady Castlemaine, were very witty. This done, they took
barge, and I with Sir J. Smith to Captain
Cox's; and there to talk, and left them and
other company to drink; while I slunk out to
Bagwell's ; and there saw her, and her mother,
and our late maid Nell, who cried for joy to see

---

[1] The second baronet of his family, and father of the Bishop
of Winchester, of the same names.

me. So to Cox's, and thence walked with Sir
J. Smith back to Redriffe; and so by water
home, and there my wife mighty angry for my
absence, and fell mightily out, but not being
certain of anything, but thinks only that Pierce
or Knipp was there, and did ask me, and, I
perceive, the boy many questions. But I did
answer her; and so, after much ado, did go to
bed, and lie quiet all night; but she had another
bout with me in the morning, but I did make
shift to quiet her, but yet she was not fully
satisfied, poor wretch! in her mind, and thinks
much of my taking so much pleasure without
her; which, indeed, is a fault, though I did not
design or foresee it when I went.

9th. Up, and to the Tower; and there find Sir
W. Coventry alone, writing down his Journal,
which, he tells me he now keeps of the material things; upon which I told him, and he is
the only man I ever told it to, I think, that I
kept it most strictly these eight or ten years;
and I am sorry almost that I told it him, it not
being necessary, nor may be convenient, to
have it known. Here he showed me the petition he hath sent to the King by my Lord
Keeper, which was not to desire any admittance
to employment, but submitting himself therein

humbly to his Majesty ; but prayed the removal
of his displeasure, and that he might be set
free.   He tells me that my Lord Keeper did
acquaint the King with the substance of it, not
showing him the petition ; who answered that
he was disposing of his employments, and when
that was done, he might be led to discharge
him : and this is what he expects, and what he
seems to desire.   But by this discourse he was
pleased to take occasion to show me and read
to me his account, which he hath kept by him
under his own hand, of all his discourse, and
the King's answers to him, upon the great business of my Lord Clarendon, and how he had
first moved the Duke of York with it twice, at
good distance, one after another, but without
success ; showing me thereby the simplicity and
reasons of his so doing, and the manner of it ;
and the King's accepting it, telling him that he
was not satisfied in his management, and did
discover some dissatisfaction against him for
his opposing the laying aside of my Lord
Treasurer, at Oxford, which was a secret the
King had not discovered.   And really I was
mighty proud to be privy to this great transaction, it giving me great conviction of the noble
nature and ends of Sir W. Coventry in it, and

considerations in general of the consequences of great men's actions, and the uncertainty of their estates, and other very serious considerations. To the Office, where we sat all the morning, and after dinner by coach to my cousin Turner's, thinking to have taken up the young ladies; but The. was let blood to-day; and so my wife and I towards the King's play-house, and by the way found Betty Turner, and Bab., and Betty Pepys staying for us; and so took them all to see 'Claricilla,' which do not please me almost at all, though there are some good things in it. And so to my cousin Turner's, and there find my Lady Mordaunt, and her sister Johnson; [1] and by and by comes in a gentleman, Mr. Overbury, a pleasant man, who plays most excellently on the flagelette, a little one, that sounded as low as one of mine, and mighty pretty. Hence with my wife, and Bab., and Betty Pepys, and W. Hewer, whom I carried all this day with me, to my cousin Stradwick's, where I have not been ever since my brother Tom died, there being some differ-ence between my father and them, upon the account of my cousin Scott; and I glad of this opportunity of seeing them, they being good

[1] Her maiden sister.

and substantial people, and kind. Here met my cousin Roger and his wife, and my cousin Turner, and here, which I never did before, I drank a glass, of a pint, I believe, at one draught, of the juice of oranges, of whose peel they make comfits; and here they drink the juice as wine, with sugar, and it is very fine drink; but it being new, I was doubtful whether it might not do me hurt. Having staid awhile, my wife and I back, with my cousin Turner, &c., to her house. There we took our leaves of my cousin Pepys, who goes with his wife and two daughters for Impington to-morrow. They are very good people, and people I love, and am obliged to, and shall have great pleasure in their friendship, and particularly in hers, she being an understanding and good woman.

12*th*. With great content spent all the morning looking over the Navy accounts of several years, and the several patents of the Treasurers. W. Hewer and myself towards Westminster; and there he carried me to Nott's, the famous bookbinder, that bound for my Lord Chancellor's library: and here I did take occasion for curiosity to bespeak a book to be bound, only that I might have one of his binding. To Graye's Inn: and, at the next door, at a cook-shop of

Howe's acquaintance, we bespoke dinner, it being now two o'clock; and in the meantime he carried us into Graye's Inn, to his chamber, where I never was before; and it is very pretty, and little, and neat, as he was always. And so, after a little stay, and looking over a book or two there, we carried a piece of my Lord Coke[1] with us, and to our dinner, where, after dinner, he read at my desire a chapter in my Lord Coke about perjury, wherein I did learn a good deal touching oaths, and so away to the Patent Office,[2] in Chancery Lane, where his brother Jack, being newly broke by running in debt, and growing an idle rogue, he is forced to hide himself; and W. Howe do look after the Office. Here I did set a clerk to look out some things for me in their books, while W. Hewer and I to the Crown Office,[3] where we met with several good things that I most wanted, and did take short notes of the dockets, and so back to the Patent Office, and did the like there, and by candle-light ended. And so home, where, thinking to meet my wife with content, after my pains all this day, I find her in her closet, alone, in the dark, in a hot fit of

---

[1] Coke's Institutes.   [2] The Rolls.
[3] In the Temple, where it is still kept.

railing against me : but, what with my high
words, and slighting, I did at last bring her to
very good and kind terms, poor heart!

13*th*. Up, and to the Tower, to see Sir W.
Coventry, and with him talking of business of
the Navy, all alone, an hour, he taking physic.
And so away to the Office, where all the morning, and then home to dinner, with my people,
and so to the Office again, and there all the
afternoon till night, when comes, by mistake,
my cousin Turner and her two daughters, which
love such freaks, to eat some anchovies and
ham of bacon with me, instead of noon, at dinner, when I expected them. But, however, I
had done my business before they come, and so
was in good humor enough to be with them, and
so home to them to supper, being pleased to see
Betty Turner, which hath something mighty
pretty. But that which put me in good humor,
both at noon and night, is the fancy that I am
this day made a Captain of one of the King's
ships, Mr. Wren having this day sent me the
Duke of York's commission to be Captain of
The Jerzy, in order to my being of a Court-
martial for examining the loss of The Defy-
ance, and other things; which do give me
occasion of much mirth, and may be of some

use to me, at least I shall get a little money for
the time I have it; it being designed that I
must really be a Captain to be able to sit in this
Court. They staid till about eight at night,
and then away, and my wife to read to me, and
then to bed in mighty good humor, but for my
eyes.

April 30*th*. Up, and by coach to the coachmaker's: and there I do find a great many ladies sitting in the body of a coach that must be
ended by to-morrow: they were my Lady Marquis of Winchester,[1] Bellassis,[2] and other great
ladies, eating of bread and butter, and drinking
ale. I to my coach, which is silvered over,
but no varnish yet laid on, so I put it in a way
of doing; and myself, about other business, and
particularly to see Sir W. Coventry, with whom
I talked a good while to my great content; and
so to other places — among others, to my tailor's:
and then to the belt-maker's, where my belt
cost me 55*s*. of the color of my new suit: and

[1] Isabella, daughter of William Howard, Viscount Stafford,
third wife to John Powlett, fifth Marquis of Winchester.

[2] John Lord Bellassis was thrice married: first, to Jane,
daughter of Sir Robert Boteler, of Woodhall, Herts; secondly, to Ann, daughter of Sir Robert Crane, of Chilton, Suffolk;
thirdly, to Lady Anne Powlett, daughter of the above-named
Marquis of Winchester (by his second wife, Lady Honora de
Burgh), and who is the person referred to by Pepys.

here, understanding **that** the mistress of the
house, an oldish woman in a hat, hath some
water good for the eyes, **she did dress** me, making **my** eyes smart most horribly, and **did** give
me a **little glass of it, which I will use,** and
hope it will do me **good.** So to the cutler's,
and there did give Tom, who was with me all
day, a sword cost **me 12s. and a belt** of my
own ; and sent my **own silver-hilt** sword a-gild-
ing against to-morrow. **This** morning I did visit
Mr. Oldenburgh,[1] **and did see** the instrument
for perspective made **by Dr.** Wren,[2] of which I
have one making by **Browne ; and** the sight of
this do please me mightily. **At** noon **my** wife
came **to me at my tailor's, and I sent** her home,
and myself **and Tom** dined at Hercules Pillars ;
and so about **our business again,** and particularly **to Lilly's, the** varnisher, about my prints,
whereof some of them are pasted upon the
boards, and to my full content. Thence to the
frame-maker's, one Norris, in Long Acre, who
**showed me several forms of frames, which were
pretty, in little bits of** mouldings, to choose **pat-**

---

1 Henry Oldenburgh, Secretary of the Royal Society.

2 A description of an instrument invented many years before, by Sir Christopher Wren, for drawing the outlines of any
object in perspective, is given in the *Abridgment* *of Phil.
Trans.*

terus by. This done, I to my coachmaker's, and there vexed to see nothing yet done to my coach, at three in the afternoon; but I set it in doing, and stood by till eight at night, and saw the painter varnish it, which is pretty to see how every doing it over do make it more and more yellow : and it dries as fast in the sun as it can be laid on almost ; and most coaches are, now-a-days, done so, and it is very pretty when laid on well, and not too pale, as some are, even to show the silver. Here I did make the work-men drink, and saw my coach cleaned and oiled ; and staying among poor people there in the alley, did hear them call their fat child Punch, which pleased me mightily, that word being be-come a word of common use for all that is thick and short.[1] At night home, and there find my wife hath been making herself clean against to-morrow ; and late as it was, I did send my coachman and horses to fetch home the coach to-night, and so we to supper, myself most weary with walking and standing so much, to see all things fine against to-morrow, and so to

---

[1] " *Puncheon*, the vessel, Fr. *poinçon*, perhaps so called from the *pointed* form of the staves ; the vessel bellying out in the middle, and tapering towards each end : and hence *punch* (*i. e.*, the large belly), became applied, as Pepys records, to anything thick or short." — Richardson's *Dictionary*.

bed. Meeting with Mr. Sheres, to several
places, and, among others, to buy a periwig,
but I bought none ; and also to Dancre's, where
he was about my picture of Windsor, which
is mighty pretty, and so will the prospect of
Rome be.

May 1*st*. Up betimes. Called by my tailor,
and here first put on a summer suit this year ;
but it was not my fine one of flowered tabby
vest, and colored camelott tunique, because it
was too fine with the gold lace at the bands,
that I was afraid to be seen in it ; but put on
the stuff suit I made the last year, which is now
repaired ; and so did go to the Office in it, and
sat all the morning, the day looking as if it
would be foul. At noon home to dinner, and
there find my wife extraordinary fine, with her
flowered tabby gown that she made two years
ago, now laced exceeding pretty ; and indeed,
was fine all over ; and mighty earnest to go,
though the day was very lowering ; and she
would have me put on my fine suit, which I did.
And so anon we went alone through the town
with our new liveries of serge, and the horses'
manes and tails tied with red ribbons, and the
standards gilt with varnish, and all clean, and
green reins, that people did mightily look upon

us ; and, the truth is, I did not see any coach more
pretty, though more gay than ours, all the day.
But we set out, out of humor — I because Betty,
whom I expected, was not come to go with us ;
and my wife that I would sit on the same seat
with her, which she likes not, being so fine :
and she then expected to meet Sheres, which
we did in the Pell Mell, and, against my will, I
was forced to take him into the coach, but was
sullen all day almost, and little complaisant :
the day being unpleasing, though the Park full
of coaches, but dusty and windy, and cold, and
now and then a little dribbling of rain ; and
what made it worse, there were so many hackney-coaches as spoiled the sight of the gentlemen's ;[1] and so we had little pleasure. But
here was W. Batelier and his sister in a borrowed coach by themselves, and I took them
and we to the lodge ; and at the door did give
them a syllabub, and other things, cost me 12s.,
and pretty merry. And so back to the coaches,
and there till the evening, and then home, leaving Mr. Sheres at St. James's Gate, where he
took leave of us for altogether, he being this
night to set out for Portsmouth post, in his way

---

[1] This is a little too much, considering that Samuel had so
recently set up his own carriage.

to Tangier, which **troubled** my wife mightily, **who** is mighty, though not, I think, too fond of him.

2d. (Lord's Day.) Up, and by water to **White** Hall, and there visited my Lord Sandwich, who, after about two months' **absence at** Hinchinbroke, came to town last night. I saw him, and he was very kind; and I am **glad he** is so, I having not wrote to him all the time, my eyes indeed not letting me. Here with Sir Charles Harbord, and my Lord Hinchinbroke, and Sidney, and we looked upon the picture of Tangier, designed by Charles Harbord, and drawn by Dancre, which my Lord Sandwich admires, as being the truest picture that ever he saw in his life: and it is indeed very pretty, and **I** will be at **the** cost of having one of them. Thence **with** them to White Hall, and there walked out the sermon, with one or other; and then saw the Duke of York, and he talked to **me a** little; and so away back by water home. After dinner, got my wife to read, and then by coach, she **and I,** to the Park, and there spent the evening **with much** pleasure, it proving clear after a little shower, and we mighty fine **as yesterday, and** people **mightily** pleased with **our coach, as I** perceive; but I had not on my fine suit, being really afraid to wear it, it being so fine with the gold lace, though not gay.

3*d*. **Up, and by** coach to my Lord Brouncker's, where Sir G. Carteret did meet Sir J. Minnes and me, to discourse upon Mr. Deering's business, who was directed, in the time of the war, to provide provisions at Hamburgh, by Sir G. Carteret's direction; and now Sir G. Carteret is afraid to own it, it being done without written order. But by our meeting, we do all begin to recollect enough to preserve Mr. Deering, which I think, poor, silly man ! I shall be glad of, it being too much he should suffer for endeavoring **to serve us.** Thence to St. James's, where the Duke of York was playing in the Pell Mell; and so he called **me to him** most part of the time that he played, **which** was an hour, and talked alone to **me**; and, among other things, tells me how the King will **not yet be** got to name anybody in the room of Pen, but puts **it off, for three or** four days; from whence he do **collect that** they are **brew**ing something for the Navy, but what he knows not; but **I** perceive is vexed that things **should** go so, and he hath reason; for he told me that **it is likely** they will do in this as in other things — **resolve first,** and consider **it and the fitness**

of it afterwards. Thence to White Hall, and
met with Creed, and discoursed of matters;
and I perceive by him that he makes no doubt
but that all will turn to the old religion, for
these people cannot hold things in their hands,
nor prevent its coming to that; and by his discourse he fits himself for it, and would have my
Lord Sandwich do so, too, and me. After a
little talk with him, and particularly about the
ruinous condition of Tangier, which I have a
great mind to lay before the Duke of York, before it be too late, but dare not, because of his
great kindness to Lord Middleton, we parted,
and I homeward; but called at Povy's, and
there he stopped me to dinner, there being Mr.
Williamson, the Lieutenant of the Tower,[1] Mr.
Child, and several others. And after dinner,
Povy and I together to talk of Tangier; and he
would have me move the Duke of York in it,
for it concerns him particularly, more than any,
as being the head of us; and I do think to do it.

4th. Walked with my wife in the garden,
and my Lord Brouncker with us, who is newly
come to W. Pen's lodgings; and by and by
comes Mr. Hooke; and my Lord, and he, and
I into my Lord's lodgings, and there discourse

---

[1] Sir John Robinson.

of many fine things in philosophy, to my great content.

5th. Up, and thought to have gone with Lord Brouncker to Mr. Hooke this morning betimes; but my Lord is taken ill of the gout, and says his new lodgings have infected him, he never having any symptoms of it till now. So walked to Gresham College, to tell Hooke that my Lord could not come; and so left word, he being abroad. To St. James's, and thence, with the Duke of York, to White Hall, where the Board waited on him all the morning: and so at noon with Sir Thomas Allen, and Sir Edward Scott,[1] and Lord Carlingford, to the Spanish Ambassador's,[2] where I dined the first time. The Olio not so good as Sheres'. There was at the table himself and a Spanish Countess, a good, comely, and witty lady — three Fathers and us. Discourse, good and pleasant. And here was an Oxford scholar in a Doctor of Law's gown, sent from the College where the Embassador lay, when the Court was there, to salute him before his return to Spain. This man, though a gentle sort of scholar, yet sat like a fool for want of French or Spanish, but

1 Sir Edward Scott, made LL.D. at Oxford, 1677.
2 The Conde de Dona.

knew only Latin, which he spoke like an Englishman,[1] to one of the Fathers. And by and
by he and I to talk, and the company very
merry at my defending Cambridge against Oxford : and I made much use of **my** French and
Spanish here, to my great content. But the
dinner not extraordinary at all, either for quantity or quality. Thence home to my wife, and
she read to me the epistle of Cassandra, which
is very good indeed ; and **the** better to her, because recommended **by** Sheres. So to supper,
and **to** bed.

6th. Up, and by coach to Sir W. Coventry's,
but he gone out. I by water back to the Office,
and there all the morning : then to dinner, and
then to the Office again, and anon with my wife
by coach to take the air, it being a noble day,
as far as the Green Man,[2] mightily pleased with

[1] *i. e.,* with the English pronunciation.

[2] Probably on Stroud Green, and known by the name of
Stapleton Hall, originally the residence of Sir Thomas Stapleton, of Gray's Court, Oxon, Bart. The building, on which
were his initials, with those of his wife, and the date 1609,
was afterwards converted into a public-house, with the sign
of the Green Man, and a century ago had in the front the following inscription : —

" Ye are welcome all
To Stapleton Hall."

A club, styling themselves " The Lord Mayor, Aldermen, and
Corporation of Stroud Green," formerly met annually at this

our journey, and our condition of doing it in our own coach, and so home, and to walk in the garden, and so to supper and **to** bed, my eyes being bad with writing my Journal, part of it, to-night.

28th. To St. James, where the King's being with the Duke of York prevented a meeting of the Tangier Commission. But, Lord! what a deal of sorry discourses did I hear between the King and several Lords about him here! but very mean, methought. So with Creed to the Excise Office, **and** back to White Hall, where, in the Park, Sir G. Carteret did give an account of his discourse lately, with the Commissioners of Accounts, who except against many things, but none that I find considerable : among others, that of the Officers of the Navy selling of the King's goods, and particularly my providing him with calico flags, which having been by order, and but once, when necessity, and the King's apparent profit justified it, as conformable to my particular duty, it will prove to my advantage that it **be** enquired into. Nevertheless, having **this** morning received from them a demand **of** an account of all monies within

place, which occasioned a scene similar to that of a country **wake or** fair. — Lewis's *Hist. of Islington.*

their cognizance, received and issued by me, I
was willing, upon this hint, to give myself rest,
by knowing whether their meaning therein
might reach only to my Treasurership for Tangier, or the monies employed on this occasion.
I went, therefore, to them this afternoon, to
understand what monies they meant, where
they answered me by saying, 'The eleven
months' tax, customs, and prize-money,' without mentioning, any more than I demanding,
the service they respected therein; and so,
without further discourse, we parted, upon
very good terms of respect, and with few
words, but my mind not fully satisfied about
the monies they mean. With my wife and
brother spent the evening on the water, carrying our supper with us, as high as Chelsea,
making sport with the Western bargees,[1] and
my wife and I singing, to my great content.

29*th*. The King's birth-day. To White
Hall, where all very gay; and particularly the
Prince of Tuscany very fine, and is the first
day of his appearing out of mourning, since he
came. I hear the Bishop of Peterborough[2]
preach but dully; but a good anthem of Pel-

---

[1] Still a cant term for the Thames bargemen.
[2] Joseph Henshaw; ob. 1678.

ham's. Home to dinner, and then with my wife to Hyde Park, where all the evening; great store of company, and great preparations by the Prince of Tuscany to celebrate the night with fire-works, for the King's birth-day. And so home.

30*th*. (Whitsunday.) By water to White Hall, and thence to Sir W. Coventry, where all the morning by his bed-side, he being indisposed. Our discourse was upon the notes I have lately prepared for Commanders' Instructions; but concluded that nothing will render them effectual, without an amendment in the choice of them, that they be seamen, and not gentlemen above the command of the Admiral, by the greatness of their relations at Court. Thence to White Hall, and dined with Mr. Cheffinch and his sister; whither by and by came in Mr. Progers and Sir Thomas Allen, and by and by, fine Mrs. Wells, who is a great beauty; and there I had my full gaze upon her, to my great content, she being a woman of pretty conversation. Thence to the Duke of York, who, with the officers of the Navy, made a good entrance on my draught of my new Instructions to Commanders, as well expressing his general views of a reformation among them,

as liking of my humble offers towards it.
Thence being **called by my wife,** we to the Park,
whence the rain sent us suddenly home.

31*st*. Up very betimes, and continued all the
morning with W. Hewer, upon examining and
stating my accounts, in order **to the** fitting myself **to** go **abroad beyond** sea, which the ill condition of my eyes, and my neglect for a year or
two, hath kept me behind-hand in, and so as to
render it very difficult now, and troublesome to
my mind to do it ; **but I** this day made a satis-
factory **entrauce therein.** Had another meeting
with the Duke of **York, at** White Hall, on yesterday's **work, and made a good advance : and**
so, **being** called by **my** wife, we to the Park,
Mary **Batclier,** and a Dutch gentleman, a friend
of hers, **being** with us. Thence to ' The
World's End,' a drinking-house by the Park ;
and there merry, and so **home.**

And thus ends all that **I** doubt **I** shall be
ever able to do with my own eyes in the keep-
ing of my Journal, I being not able to do it any
longer, having done now so long as to undo my
eyes almost every time that I take a pen in my
hand ; and, therefore, whatever comes of it, I
must forbear : and, therefore, resolve from this

time forward, to have it kept by my people in long hand, and must be contented to set down no more than is fit for them and all the world to know ; or, if there be any thing, I must endeavor to keep a margin in my book open, to add, here and there, a note in short-hand with my own hand.

And so I betake myself to that course, which is almost as much as to see myself go into my grave : for which, and all the discomfits that will accompany my being blind, the good God prepare me !

S. P.

MAY 31, 1669."

As has been already stated by the Secretary, failing sight compelled him to abandon his Diary ; and having obtained from the King a few months' leave of absence, he availed himself of the opportunity to visit France and Holland, being accompanied in his tour by Mistress Pepys. Upon this excursion he often looks back with lively pleasure in his correspondence and conversation. Soon after his return to England, he had the misfortune to lose his wife, who died at his house in Hart Street, London, leaving no issue. She had been ill only a few days. On the 3d of March, 1670, Pepys writes to a friend : —

" I beg you earnestly to believe that nothing but the sorrow and distraction I have been in by the death of my wife, increased by the suddenness with which it pleased God to surprise me therewith, after a voyage so full of health and content, could have forced me to so long a neglect of my private concernments ; this being, I do assure you, the very first day that my affliction, together with my daily attendance on other public occasions of his Majesty's, has suffered me to apply myself to the considering any part of my private concernments ; among which, that of my doing right to you is no small particular : and therefore, as your charity will, I hope, excuse me for my not doing it sooner, so I pray you to accept now (as late as it is) my hearty thanks for your multiplied kindness in my late affair at Aldborough ; [1] and in particular your courteous providing of your own house for my reception, had I come down ; the entertainment you were also pleased to prepare for me, together with your other great pains and charges in the preserving that interest which you had gained, in reference to his

---

[1] His unsuccessful election contest.

Royal Highness's and my Lord Howard's desire on my behalf: in all which I can give you good assurance, that not only his Royal Highness retains a thankful memory of your endeavors to serve him, but I shall take upon **me the** preserving it so with him that it may be useful to you when you shall have any occasion of asking his favor. The like I dare promise you from **my Lord** Howard, **when he** shall return; and both from them and myself make this kindness **of** yours, and the rest of **those** gentlemen **of the town who** were pleased **to concur with you, as** advantageous both to yourself and them, and to the Corporation also, **as if the business had** succeeded to the best of our wishes: and this I assure you, whether I shall ever hereafter **have** the honor of serving them in Parliament **or not,** having no reason to receive any thing with dis**satisfaction** in this whole matter, saving the particular disrespect which our noble master, the Duke of York, suffered from the beginning to the end, from **Mr.** Duke and Captain Shippman, who, I doubt not, may meet with a time of seeing their error therein. But I am extremely ashamed to find **myself** so much outdone by you in kindness, by your not suffering **me to** know the expense which this business has occasioned you ; which I again entreat you to let me do, esteeming your pains (without that of your charge) an obligation greater than I can foresee opportunity of requiting, though I shall by no means omit to endeavor it. So with a repetition of my hearty acknowledgments of all your kindness, with my service to yourself and lady, and all my worthy friends about you, I remain,

Your obliged friend and humble Servant,

S. P."

The illness of his wife prevented **Pepys** from attending the election at Aldborough, and his absence was probably the cause of his being defeated. In January, 1673, however, he was elected a member of Parliament for another borough. In the summer of the same year, the Duke of York having resigned all his employments, upon the passing of the Test Act, the King called Pepys into his own service as Secretary for the affairs of the Navy. Ten years later, he accompanied Lord Dartmouth on the expedition against Tangier ; at the same time availing himself of the opportunity of making excursions into Spain. From this expedition Pepys returned in the spring of 1684 ;

and the King having assumed the office of High
Admiral, he was, " by the Royal commands
neither sought for nor foreseen, brought to him
expressly by Lord Dartmouth from Windsor,"
constituted Secretary for the affairs of the Admiralty, which office he continued to fill during
the remainder of the reign of the Stuarts. The
curious circumstance respecting the religion of
Charles I., related by Evelyn, rests chiefly upon
the authority of our immortal diarist, to whom
King James himself had communicated it.
We are also told that when the latter was sitting to Sir Godfrey Kneller for his picture,
intended as a present to Pepys, news coming of
the Prince of Orange having landed, the King,
with the utmost composure, desired the painter
to proceed and finish the portrait, that his good
friend the Secretary might not be disappointed.
Upon the accession of William and Mary,
Pepys lost his official employments, retiring to
private life, and the enjoyment of literary society and pursuits. Of his munificence as a
patron of literature, the large number of books
dedicated to him furnish ample testimony; and
in the preface to Willoughby's Historia Pis-
cium, he is justly styled " Ingenuarum Artium
et Eruditorum Fautor et Patronus Eximius,"

16

as having contributed no fewer than sixty plates to that valuable work. In the year 1690, Pepys was arrested on a charge of being too favorable to the exiled James, but was soon released; ten years later, after having published "Memoirs relating to the State of the Navy," he abandoned his city residence, and retired to the repose and quiet of the country, seeking shelter under the roof of an old friend whose seat was at Clapham. Here, in this pleasant retreat, surrounded by attached relatives and friends, he occupied the greater part of his time in reading his favorite authors, and in corresponding with Evelyn, Charlett, and other eminent men. His brother diarist, Evelyn, who survived him for three years, in one of his letters, dated January, 1702–3, says, "Thus, what I would wish for myself and all I love, as I do Mr. Pepys, should be the old man's life as described in the distich, which you deservedly have attained: —

'Vita, Senis, libri, domus, hortus, lectus, amicus,
  Vina, Nepos inquis, mens hilaris, pietas.'

In the mean time, I feed on the past conversation I once had in York Buildings, and starve since my friend has forsaken it." After a lingering illness, Samuel Pepys, F. R. S., Secretary to the Admiralty in the reigns of Charles II. and James II., the prince of diarists, passed away, May 26, 1703, to "those temples not made with hands." George Hickes, D. D., deprived of the deanery of Worcester for refusing to take the oaths to King William, writes to Dr. Charlett, June 5, " Last night, at 9 o'clock, I did the last office for your and my good friend, Mr. Pepys, at St. Olaves Church,[1] where he was laid in a vault of his own making, by his wife and brother. The greatness of his behavior, in his long and sharp trial before his death, was in every respect answerable to his great life : and I believe no man ever went out of this world with greater contempt of it, or a more lively faith in every thing that was revealed of the world to come. I administered the Holy Sacrament twice in his illness to him, and had administered it a third time but for a sudden fit of illness that happened at the appointed time of administering of it. Twice I gave him the absolution of the Church, which he desired, and received with all reverence and comfort, and I never attended any sick or dying person, that died with so much Christian

[1] In Hart Street, London.

greatness of mind, or a more lively sense of
immortality, or so much fortitude and patience,
in so long and sharp a trial, or greater resigna-
tion to the will, which he most devoutly ac-
knowledged to be the wisdom of God: and I
doubt not but he is now a very blessed spirit
according to his motto, ' MENS CUJUSQUE, IS
EST QUISQUE.' "

Evelyn, in his Diary, uses the following language in writing of his deceased friend and
fellow-diarist : —

" *May 26th.* This day died Mr. Sam Pepys,
a very worthy, industrious, and curious person,
none in England exceeding him in knowledge of
the navy, in which he had passed through all the
most considerable offices, Clerk of the Acts and
Secretary of the Admiralty, all which he per-
formed with great integrity. When K. James
II. went out of England, he laid down his office,
and would serve no more, but withdrawing himself from all public affairs, he lived at Clapham
with his partner Mr. Hewer, formerly his clerk,
in a very noble house and sweet place, where
he enjoyed the fruit of his labors in great prosperity. He was universally beloved, hospitable, generous, learned in many things, skilled
in music, a very great cherisher of learned men,

of whom he had the conversation. His library
and collection of other curiosities were of the
most considerable, the models of ships especially.
Besides what he published of an account of the
navy, as he found and left it, he had for divers
years under his hand the History of the Navy,
or *Navalia*, as he called it : but how far advanced, and what will follow of his, is left, I
suppose, to his sister's son Mr. Jackson, a
young gentleman whom Mr. Pepys had edu-
cated in all sorts of useful learning, sending
him to travel abroad, from whence he returned
with extraordinary accomplishments, and worthy to be heir. Mr. Pepys had been for near
40 years so much my particular friend, that
Mr. Jackson sent me complete mourning, desiring me to be one to hold up the pall at his
magnificent obsequies, but my indisposition
hindered me from doing him this last office."

By his will, our annalist bequeathed to Magdalen College, Cambridge, an accumulation of
literary treasures. Of these, the most conspic-
uous portion was his library. Fortunately for
posterity, although Pepys was quite a Sir Pier-
cie Shafton in his way, and never formed a
complete opinion of any man without due consideration of his clothes, he was something of a

bibliomaniac, albeit he had not the disease to
the same extent as Southey's friend, whom, the
poet relates, one day showed him his small and
curious hoard. "Have you ever seen a copy
of this book?" asked the bibliomaniac, with
every volume that he placed in Southey's
hands; and when the poet replied that he had
not, always rejoined, with a look and tone of
triumphant delight, "I should have been exceedingly sorry if you had!" Pepys, with no
inconsiderable expenditure of time and money,
gathered together a remarkably good and interesting collection, comprising not only many
curiosities of early typography, but copious
specimens of the fugitive literature of his day.
Six large folio volumes, for instance, are filled
with broadsides, ballads, and songs of every
description, each of which is now almost unique;
while the marketable value of the whole
has been computed by thousands of dollars.
From this collection Bishop Percy chiefly de-
rived his Reliques of Ancient English Poetry.
Pepys thought there was "nothing like leath-
er," and so his literary treasures were all en-
cased in the choicest bindings in vogue at the
close of the seventeenth century. Early in life,
he resolved on no account to fill more than a

certain number of "presses," i. e., bookcases ;
and accordingly, as he acquired any valuable
volume fitted for a niche in his library, he
weeded his shelves of its least dignified or rare
specimens to make way for his new acquisi-
tions. At the beginning of each year, too,
with the aid of Mistress Pepys and her maid,
he was wont to "set them up" afresh ; and we
are favored in the Diary with particular records
of the appearance which the "presses" made
at any one period compared with the show of
the previous year. This choice and curious
collection, thus gleaned together in the course
of thirty years, our friend Samuel at length
bequeathed to Magdalen College, on conditions
which included its preservation in the selfsame
plight in which he had left it. The "presses"
were to be kept in an apartment exclusively
devoted to themselves, and their contents were
neither to be increased nor diminished by a
single volume, but were to remain forever in
their original state and form. As he willed, so
it has been. In a certain room of what was
once called "the new building" of Magdalen
College, and on the exterior wall of which the
visitor could read the inscription, "BIBLIO-
THECA PEPYSIANA," was this unique collec-

tion for many years deposited, until, at a
recent period, it was removed to a handsome
apartment in the lodge lately erected for
the master of the college. There, among the
videnda of the university, Pepys's valuable
library and fine collection of prints, paintings,
and manuscrips may now be seen, the "presses"
and their quaint contents being just as they
were left by the annalist in 1703, the former in
all the glory of black mahogany and glazed
doors, the latter in their original bindings and
in their original order.

In the Pepysian library were six large volumes filled with writing in short hand, which
remained undeciphered, if not unnoticed, till
some fifty years ago, when they attracted the
attention of persons competent to estimate their
value, and the cipher was soon after submitted
to a Cambridge scholar for interpretation.
The contents of the half dozen volumes were
soon translated, and were found to be a perfect
treasure trove, being nothing less than a faithful
and particular Diary of Samuel Pepys's life
and conversation from the 1st of January,
1660, to the 31st of May, 1669. The Diary,
or rather a large selection from it, was first
published in 1825, in five volumes, and the

speedy sale of two large editions proved how accurately its interest had been estimated by its editor, Richard Lord Braybrooke, who has collateral claims on the blood of Mr. Secretary Pepys. In 1848, a third edition, considerably enlarged, was published, followed ere long by a fourth, in the preface to which the editor says, "The Memoirs of Samuel Pepys, and the History of his Short-hand Diary, have been so long well known to the literary world, that the fourth edition of the work comprised in the following pages can hardly require any formal or lengthened introduction. It should, however, be explained, that as the edition of 1848, which had found more general favor than its predecessors, was already out of print, the publisher strongly urged that the book should again be brought forth under my auspices, and I have ventured to accede to his request. So true is the French couplet, —

> 'On revient toujours,
> A ses premiers amours.'"

In 1854 another edition appeared; another was published four years later; and in 1865 the seventh edition, from which our extracts are taken, was issued.

To the diarists of past days the world is indebted for much of its information; and certainly no other class of writings have added so much to what Dr. Johnson calls "the gayety of mankind." Among the ancients, we have the Memorabilia of Xenophon, the Commentaries of Cæsar, and the Journal of Nearchus, Alexander's admiralty works which may be said to belong to this order of composition. Concerning the heroic age of modern Europe, we have the Memoirs and Chronicles of Commines and Froissart, the romances of chivalry, and the invaluable records contained in the humorous and more familiar tales of Geoffry Chaucer. For our knowledge of the period over which the last of the Stuarts reigned, we are chiefly indebted to John Evelyn, Samuel Pepys, Thomas Rugge, author of the Diurnall, from which we have frequently quoted in our notes, and to the memoirs and journals of Lord Clarendon, Mrs. Lucy Hutchinson, and Lady Fanshawe. Among these very considerable memorials of that age, none will compare with the Diary of the quaint and garrulous Samuel. No autobiography of which we have any knowledge makes the least perceptible approach to it. Rousseau's Confessions will bear no kind of comparison. Perhaps the reflections of Silvio Pellico in his prison supply a somewhat nearer match; but the two productions are hardly homogeneous enough to be compared. It is certainly one of the pleasantest books we have ever taken up, and we trust the possessors of this little *brochure* will be of the same opinion after having perused the examples which have been segregated from the worthy Secretary's four volumes. We have quoted liberally, because we were anxious that our readers should share with us the pleasure of looking upon so admirable a picture of one of the most interesting periods of English history, — the first nine years of Charles **II.'s reign,** — and because, having spoken so highly of its many beauties, we are bound in a manner, as the lawyers say, " to instruct our averments."

We cannot better take leave of our annalist and his inimitable Diary than in the words of Francis Jeffrey, who, in one of his delightful essays, **says,** " And now we have done with Mr. Pepys. There is trash enough, no doubt, in his journal — trifling facts and silly observations. **But we** can scarcely **say that** we wish it a page shorter, and are **of the** opinion that there is **very little of it which does not** help us

to understand the character of his times and
his contemporaries better than we should ever
have done without it, and make us feel more
assured that we comprehend the great historical events of the age, and the people who bore
a part in them.   Independent of instruction
altogether, too, there is no denying that it is
very entertaining thus to be transported into
the very heart of a time so long gone by, and
to be admitted into the domestic intimacy, as
well as the public councils, of a man of great
activity and circulation in the reign of Charles
II.   Reading this book seems to us to be
quite as good as living with Mr. Samuel
Pepys in his proper person; and though the
court scandal may be detailed with more grace
and vivacity in the Mémoires de Grammont,
we have no doubt that even this part of his
multifarious subject is treated with far greater
fidelity and fairness before us, while it gives us
more clear and undistorted glimpses into the
true English life of the times — for the court
was substantially foreign — than all the other
memorials of them that have come down to our
own."

INDEX.

(253)

17